SON OF THE THUNDERCLOUD

SON OF THE THUNDERCLOUD

Easterine Kire

SPEAKING
TIGER

SPEAKING TIGER PUBLISHING PVT. LTD
4381/4, Ansari Road, Daryaganj
New Delhi 110002

First published in hardback by Speaking Tiger 2016

ISBN: 978-93-86338-14-3
e-ISBN: 978-93-863382-0-4

10 9 8 7 6 5 4 3 2 1

The moral right of the author has been asserted.

Typeset in Sabon Roman by SÜRYA, New Delhi
Printed at Sanat Printers, Kundli

For JJ and Isaac,
13 years

CONTENTS

PROLOGUE

'*In a small village of the Angamis, there lived an old woman. She was the saddest person alive in those hills. Many years ago, a tiger had killed her husband and seven sons, and her heart had still not healed. She spent long, lonely days waiting for the hour when she would join her loved ones in death.*

'*One afternoon, the woman was drying paddy outside her house when, all of a sudden, the sun disappeared and a raindrop fell on her from the sky. She became pregnant and gave birth to a son. She was happy again, and the son grew up to be a mighty warrior who avenged his father and seven brothers.*'

'*When did it happen? Where are the woman and her son now?*'

'Oh, it happened a very long time ago. And it will happen again.'

'I don't understand!'

'You will, little one, when the time is right. Now go to sleep.'

1

PELE

When he was born, he was named Pelevotso, but when he was growing up, everyone called him Pele. Except his grandmother, who would say, 'His full name is actually Pelevotso. We must remember that.'

She was his father's mother, and she had walked half a day from her hut at the edge of a forest to see the newborn. Ever since her husband died in a hunt, she had lived alone, collecting jungle herbs to heal sick and wounded animals and men. People called her 'the solitary one'.

That afternoon, she had held the infant in her lap and said, 'We'll call him Pelevotso.'

'It's a big name for a child. Are you sure he can carry it?' her daughter-in-law asked.

'I know it is a big name to carry. It means faithful to the end, and that is not easy. But we cannot continue to give our children safe and insignificant names. It is a way of stopping them from living powerful lives, and making sure they don't wander too far from the village.'

'It's because we love them that we don't want them to wander too far from us,' her daughter-in-law said.

'Yes, and that also stops them from living a life of heroism and wisdom,' the grandmother replied. 'Pray that your son understands the meaning of his name and lives a good life. He's destined to wander.'

Her son and daughter-in-law agreed to the name out of respect for the elder. But after she went away, they shortened it to Pele.

～

Pele's village was called Nialhuo; it was set on the western hills. Below the hills, there were many forests where the young men learned to hunt, and two small rivers where they fished and bathed. The older people of the village would often say, 'It's the best place to live in. We are blessed. Our young should not think there are lands better than this to build a home. They belong here, they must take the place of their ancestors.' They feared that if the young were not taught to love the village, it would soon be abandoned. They had seen it happen around them.

Everyone knew of the two ghost villages. The first had become a very rich village; abundant harvests filled the granaries till they began to overflow. People would leave half their harvests to rot in the fields, because there was no more space in the village granaries. Soon they grew careless about the taboo that said that every village must keep aside some grain after the harvest as seed-grain.

One afternoon, when they were on their way back from their fields, the villagers saw black clouds of field mice swarming over their granaries and homes. Not one house or granary had been spared, and people had to abandon the village, because it is taboo to live in a village when its food stores have been wiped out by animals and insects.

In the second village, the members of the upper clan killed a man from the lower clan in a drunken brawl. The murder led to a war between the two clans and, by the end of the seventh day, so much blood had been spilt in the village that it became taboo to live there. The women and children filled their baskets with their belongings and walked out, weeping loudly. The men followed them with guilty hearts; they knew that if they had stopped the first killings they would not have lost their homes.

Pele grew up in a household that knew the taboos and taught him to respect them. His parents were content that he understood their beliefs and helped them in the fields and in the house. Their only moments of anxiety arose when his grandmother came on her yearly visits, before her death, and spoke to him about opening his heart to the unknown. They were happy that he loved his grandmother, but they did not want him to be influenced by her. She had chosen a difficult life, far from the village and all her relatives. That was not a life they wanted for their son.

When he was no longer a boy, Pele's mother found him a good woman to marry, and they were soon blessed with a child. Everything seemed to be going well, and Pele and his wife tilled their field and reaped a good harvest in their first two years together. Along with the other members of their village, they expected life to continue like this. No one was prepared for the famine that came without warning. Only when it happened did the elders remember an old seer who had seen famine before and had predicted that it would return in their lifetime, sweeping across the hills after a single season of failed rains.

Village after village was affected by the famine; people left their ancestral homes to leave for far-off lands where they could find food and water. In Nialhuo, the food ran out after a month of being rationed. The drought killed off the children first, and then many of the women, one by one. When his wife and children died, Pele bolted his house and decided to leave the village. His parents and other relatives begged him not to go.

'We understand your grief. But stay with us. Help us live,' they said. So he stayed, but as a stranger to the dead village that they insisted on calling home.

In a few days, the supplies of food ran out in every household and Pele's parents died within hours of each other. He buried them in the courtyard of their house. Now there was no reason for him to stay. With no more than the clothes upon his back and a hunting knife, he walked away. He never once looked back.

2

GREY EARTH

When he had been travelling for two weeks, perhaps more, he could not be sure, Pele came to the base of a black mountain. His feet hurt and his white canvas shoes were brown with dust. There had been no big roads, just narrow mountain paths that he followed up and down until they brought him to some human settlement or a solitary dwelling. He would partake of the hospitality of the starving inhabitants and continue on his journey.

Everywhere he stopped, he was told he should go to the Village of Weavers. Rumour had it that there was enough food and water to be found there. They might let him stay and build a home. In the last habitation where he was told this, a man gave him detailed directions to the Village of Weavers.

Pele decided to go, if only to keep travelling. He did not know if he wanted to build a home. He did not know what he wanted; except hunger, thirst and physical pain, he felt nothing. The journey could take him anywhere, or nowhere.

The mountain lay between him and the Village of Weavers. It was a hard climb and when he reached the top, the sun had begun to sink low on the horizon. Pele stopped in his tracks and looked around him. He had never seen such desolation in all his travels. Before him stretched miles of barrenness. The earth was so dry that the soil no longer looked like soil. It had cracked apart, every brittle vein and ligament exposed, looking more like sun-dried sponge with big holes running through the sod. The brown colour had gone from the soil and if the traveller were to describe it, he would call it grey, death-grey. It had long given up the struggle to sustain any form of life. His eyes scanned the horizon for people, though he asked himself how anyone could possibly survive here.

To the east, he saw a knot of houses. But as he began his descent, he saw that they were dilapidated sheds crumbling to the ground, the few remaining posts vainly holding up the overhanging roofs of thatch. They looked as desolate as the dead fields. Everything looked abandoned. He decided to spend the night in one of the ruins and set out early for whatever else lay in his path. He was some distance from the base of the mountain when he saw movement. Two dark figures emerged out of the sheds and stopped by a large rock, looking up at him. Were they human or were they spirits? He could not tell. His pace slowed down; he was surprised that he could still feel fear after weeks of lonely travel. He watched as the figures began to move again, almost gliding through the air rather than walking on the dead earth. And as they came closer, something calmed him a little.

It was only when they spoke that he realized they were human.

'You have come far, traveller. We have no food, but you may shelter in our house. That is our way. We never turn a traveller away and it will soon be night, so you may be our guest.'

Pele looked at them, from one to the other. They were covered in coarse black cloth from shoulder to knee. From their gentle ways and the thin voice, he guessed they were women, though there was nothing else about them to tell their gender.

The woman who had spoken was so gaunt that he could see the shape of her bones under the paper-thin flesh. In fact, the shinbone of one leg was completely exposed and had calloused into the same grey colour as the earth around their dwelling.

They came closer to him, and he struggled not to show

his shock at their pitiful state. 'Who are you? What place is this that I have come to?' he asked softly.

'This was once the village of Noune, traveller, before a great famine destroyed our people. Our fields are no longer cultivable as you have seen; they haven't been for many years, from a time when we were not born. Our elders told us that our newborn babies died because their mothers' milk dried up and there was nothing else to give them. It was really more merciful that way, for if they had lived, they would only have had to suffer terrible starvation for much longer. They say that those of us who survived have done so because of the great hope of the ancestors who used to say that our ancient misfortune will end when the Son of the Thundercloud is born. Everything will be transformed then. He will bring rain and mist that softens the soil, and the earth will sprout grain and grass again. There will be food and life. This is why we have been kept alive.'

Pele had seen famine, but this was unimaginable desolation. The earth he stood on must have been dead for a very long time. He tried to recollect if he had ever heard of a great famine of the past from his parents or grandparents, but he could not remember.

'Please tell me, if you can, how long has this famine lasted?' he asked.

'Seven hundred years,' the first woman answered.

'And how old are you then?'

'I am four hundred years old and my sister is twenty years younger.'

Pele stood rooted to the spot, unable to breathe for a moment. He simply stared at the women, mere skeletons covered in tattered cloth. They both had stringy hair that had not been combed in years. Their eyes were about the only things alive in them, glimmering faintly with expectation as they answered his questions.

When he spoke, it was a whisper. 'How have you survived all this time? What have you found to eat when there has been no food for so long?'

The two women shivered and held each other's hands. They were silent for a long time and Pele worried that he had said something very painful to them. They must have seen all their loved ones die one by one without being able to do anything to help them. He regretted asking the last question and lowered his gaze. But a small sound escaped them that sounded almost like a giggle. He dared to look at them again, and saw that they were laughing softly.

'Hope, sir, we have been living on hope. Every morning when we wake up, we eat hope, and so we live to see another day,' the younger woman said.

Her sister asked, 'Tell me, traveller, do you have any knowledge of the Son of the Thundercloud? Do they speak of him where you come from?'

The question, and their eerie laughter, caught Pele completely off guard and he lied, 'No, I have never heard of him.'

3

DANCE OF THE STARS

'What is your name, traveller?' the older woman asked.

She was the taller of the two, and less spectral, despite her painfully gaunt appearance. As for her sister, Pele thought that someone could easily mistake her for a length of crushed black velvet cloth blowing in the wind. Not that there was anything of the finesse of velvet about her, but it was the way she looked so ephemeral, like the wind would blow her away at any moment if it blew just a little hard. He looked from one to the other and marvelled that he was having a conversation with them at all. But there was something about them, a childlike spirit and openness, that had disarmed him. Already, he had lost the initial fear one has of the unknown.

'My name?' he said, as though he had forgotten it. Was he still himself, the heartbroken man who had left his home to travel through this parched land to nowhere in particular? Or had he become someone else and did not know? He looked at the women. They were still waiting for his answer, and now he could see their eyes, dark winter-night eyes that waited expectantly, as if his name would give meaning to their existence. There was innocence in the eyes that watched and waited upon his every word. There was nothing to fear here.

'My name is Pele. I am on my way to the Village of Weavers. I never expected to find anyone here. Had I not seen you two, I would have sheltered for the night in one of the broken houses and walked on. Then when I noticed some movement and saw two figures in the ruins...I might have taken a different path altogether.'

'Yes, we know,' said the tall one 'No one comes near because they think we are the spirits of our ancestors haunting this place. But you see for yourself, we are flesh and blood. We are not spirits, not yet.'

Pele saw her smile as she said this, and he felt sorry for them in a way he had never felt sorry for anyone. He wondered why they should make him feel so. Yet he also felt wonderment at their life: eating hope and staying alive! They didn't seem to be sorry for themselves, and the expectation in their eyes was nothing short of wondrous. They didn't mind their ghostly existence, so strong was their desire to see the Son of the Thundercloud. Everything else had become unimportant to them. And that made him doubly curious.

'Do you know how far the Village of Weavers is from here?' he asked them. He had to confess that he had lost track of where he was, and that he could no longer make sense of the directions he had been given to the village.

'You must go to the Village of Weavers. But it has moved since the time you were given directions,' the older woman said. 'The stars pull it along with them, and it is even further east now than when you were first told of it.'

'How do you know this?' Pele had to ask.

'Because we watch the stars every night, and every night they move a little southeast. But you wouldn't know because you spend your nights sleeping.'

'We will show you tonight if you can bear to stay awake,' the younger one offered.

'And if I don't stay here and go on, is there another village where I could shelter?' Pele asked, for he had remembered that they had no food.

'Not for a whole day, and you would risk running into the wolves that attack anything on these hills.'

'I'll stay here then.'

'It is a good decision,' the women said.

～

They led him to the abandoned ruins, and he followed them into the house they lived in.

Sheaves of dried herbs hung on the walls of the first room. Except for that, the house was completely bare. There were just two mats on the floor. They pulled one over to him.

'No, that is your bed. You won't have anything to sleep on if you give me that!' he protested.

But the first woman laughed and said, 'We don't sleep much. We don't waste time sleeping. He could come at any time. But you need your sleep. Or you could stay awake and watch the stars with us.'

Pele took the mat and spread his own blanket over it. How strange they were, he thought, surprising him every moment. Maybe he should do what they did in order to see what they saw. From where he was, he could see the sky through the many holes in the roof. Stretching himself on the mat, he lay down and adjusted his eyes to the darkness. At first the skies above him were not completely dark. They were cloudy and unpromising. But after some time, the clouds moved westward, and the black track of sky gleamed faintly.

'There!' they cried triumphantly, 'Just watch closely!'

Pele looked at the skies and they seemed no different than they did on all the other evenings he had looked on them. Then, suddenly, the stars appeared, not as fixed pinpoints of light, but as celestial bodies moving in harmony with each other, like in an orchestrated dance. And the two women were right, the stars were moving eastward, and even as he lay there on the hard floor, he could feel them pull the earth with them. It was marvelous, the way they swept slowly eastward, millions of stars all at once, and how everything obeyed. He knew, as if he could see it all, that rocks were shifting and river courses were being redirected and whole mountains were sliding east.

'What is this?' he asked in a loud whisper.

'Hush, hush. Feel it, just feel it for now. Don't talk.'

Though it felt as though it had gone on for a long time, the whole event had lasted only a few minutes, and when it was over, the clouds came back into place and everything was as before. Pele's first reaction was to get up and ask the women to tell him about it, but a terrible weariness came over him, and he fell fast asleep.

4

SOME CALL IT MORNING

Pele woke up and tried to remember where he was. A hazy blue light had entered from the broken roof and filled the house completely. He watched the haze swirling through the interior of the house. His bed, the cold floor, was hard as stone, but he felt surprisingly rested. Had he slept like that any other night, his back would have let him know the next morning and well into the afternoon. Not today. He felt well and ready for whatever the day held for him.

Memory returned to him all of a sudden. The women! Where were they? Had he dreamed it all? The last thing he remembered was watching the stars pull the earth eastward. How ridiculous that sounded in the light of day. Where were those crazy sisters? He got to his feet quickly and looked around. There was no one inside. The fireplace had not seen a fire for many days, perhaps years.

'I've got to get out of here!' he cried as he picked up his bag and ran out of the house. But when he came outside, there they were, at the edge of the land, looking over the top and beckoning him to come. So they were real after all, but he could not have seen the stars moving, or had he? Pele went over to join them, and the tall one pointed to the earth below them. There was a deep chasm before him that certainly had not been there yesterday. The blue haze hovered above it.

'What! What—how did that happen?' Pele stammered.

'Remember the stars last night? They were pulling the earth eastward; you saw it too. This is their work.' The older sister pointed to the abyss in front of them. The fibrous tentacles of roots and subterranean matter was stretched tautly between the two sides. Sharp ends of rocks jutted upward. A man could break his neck if he fell into that, thought Pele.

'What will happen now?' he asked.

'We don't know. The stars do this sometimes. After some weeks, when they pull again, the portion that is left behind moves forward and joins the other side. Maybe they will do that.'

'So what we saw last night was real?' Pele wanted confirmation. 'Please tell me what is happening.'

'What did you see, Pele?'

'The stars in the skies moving and pulling so violently that the earth on which we lay was pulled eastward.'

'That is what you saw and felt. That is what happened.'

'But why? What purpose will it serve?' Pele asked.

The sisters shivered again, laughing their secret little laugh.

'One day, maybe you will find out.'

'Is this some sort of preparation for the coming of the Son of the Thundercloud?' Pele asked even as he scolded himself inwardly: *Now* you *are beginning to sound like them!*

'Perhaps it is. For nothing has meaning without him, and nothing is worth living for apart from him.'

And quite unexpectedly, without any warning, a great sadness swept over Pele. The vast emptiness of the land around him seemed to enter his heart. He knew he would have no answer if he was asked the question: what is worth living for? Then he collected himself. He should leave.

As they stood there, the haze lifted a little, but the sky was overcast. Then distant thunder rolled over the hills.

'What was that sound?' the second sister asked. 'It's like nothing I have heard before.'

Pele was taken aback at first. Surely she knew it was thunder? But she looked confused, and when Pele looked at the older sister he saw the same confusion.

'It's thunder. It means it's going to rain soon. You two should probably go indoors and I should probably get going,' Pele said.

But the second sister's reaction to his words startled him. She jumped up and down and shrieked, 'Rain! Sister, did you hear? He said it will rain!'

Her sister looked at him with the same excitement and explained, 'We haven't seen rain since we were born!'

'That is crazy!' he said. 'It's unbelievable! How can anyone live four hundred years upon this earth and not see rain?'

But something about them convinced him that they were telling the truth.

'You should go indoors for shelter. That rain sounds ugly. You might just be washed away if you are not careful.'

'What about you? Shouldn't you take shelter too? There's not another village for a long while on the road you are going to take.'

Pele looked up at the sky. A mass of thick, dark clouds had built up over them. He couldn't outrun this rain. He would have to stay back and wait for it to pass.

'Let's get back to the house, quick,' he urged. 'I'll have to repair your roof before the rain pelts us.'

He ran back to pull out whatever he could find: old sheets of perforated tarpaulin, thatch so old that it fell apart when he pulled it, jute bags, and wood and broken bricks to hold them down. He spread the jute over the gaping holes in the roof, then he pulled the tarpaulin over the jute and secured it with the wood and bricks. That would have to do, because there was no other material he could use. The sisters ran back excitedly, looking like a pair of happy children. The more time he spent with them, the more human they appeared to him.

'Better stay under this portion of roof,' he said, indicating the part that he had covered as best as he could. Obediently they made their way there. The younger one ran and grabbed her mat and spread it on the floor. She lay down and watched the clouds as they gathered menacingly over the valley.

'I'm so glad I lived long enough to see this!' she shouted joyfully. Pele could not understand how anyone could live as long as the sisters claimed to have lived and not see rain. But there was no time to think about that as the storm of the century slammed into them, blowing away the crumbling houses that still stood around them and battering at the roof Pele had just made. The sisters cowered together under the flimsy shelter, and Pele looked through the cracks in the walls. The storm was terrifically strong. Raindrops as big as fists slammed into the stone-hard ground. The dry earth made sucking sounds as the water ran into it, filling it up, running deep inside the soil, getting into the countless cracks and fissures, threatening to flood.

It rained all morning, heavily, fiercely, as though the rivers of heaven were emptying onto the earth. It was seven-hundred-year-old rain. The bottomless chasm that had opened up the night before drew in all the water and saved the village from a terrible flood.

5

SON OF THE THUNDERCLOUD

When the storm finally passed, Pele and the sisters crept out of the house to see what damage had been done. All the other houses had been flattened and the debris washed away completely. But it wasn't destruction they saw around them. Everything looked clean and fresh, as if the earth was newly born and creation would start all over again. The sponge-like stony soil had been softened by the rain, and the large holes in it had closed over. Pele was surprised to see that the deluge had taken everything away but not the seed grain from the vanished ruins. It lay in the countless crevices that were already beginning to close. Perhaps the seeds would come alive and grow, even if they were seven hundred years old. The thought brought a smile to Pele.

He looked at the two women. They were going around and looking at everything that could be used as evidence of the rain. Like giggling, happy children they cupped the rainwater that had collected in empty pitchers and slowly let it trickle away between their thin fingers. They looked at their reflections in the puddles, and laughed and laughed. One of them, the younger one, scooped up water from an old aluminum pot and drank it. She was sorry immediately after, as the water made her cough until she was bent over, holding her throat.

Pele anxiously ran to her and asked, 'Are you alright? You shouldn't drink rainwater. It's not clean. You have to boil it first, you know.'

'I—I was too happy,' she gasped. The coughing subsided and she assured Pele that she was fine. Pele was suddenly struck by the transformation in the ancient sisters. The deluge had opened up something in them. They looked younger and more human now. Their features appeared clearer, and they did not seem so very thin anymore.

'You two,' he began, and stopped because he did not know how to say it. He tried again, and blurted out, 'You're changing!'

'Yes we are. It's one of the promises—that the latter rain will replenish the earth and all its creatures.'

'It's amazing. You're growing younger before my eyes!'

'Well, we might not grow all that much younger. After all, four hundred years is very, very old!' the tall one laughed, and something about the manner in which she threw her head back as she laughed made Pele unaccountably happy.

'You must tell me your names,' he said. It struck him now that he had been very rude and not even bothered to ask their names.

The sisters did not seem to mind. 'I am Kethonuo,' the older one said, 'and my sister is Siedze. We have lived all our lives waiting for the rain. It is the sign for his birth—the Son of the Thundercloud is here.'

Pele considered the two names: Kethonuo meant truth, and Siedze was the future—no, it was more than that; it meant a future full of hope.

'Come, we must all leave for the Village of Weavers now,' Kethonuo said, suddenly sounding anxious, and Siedze began to walk quickly back towards their shell of a house, muttering, 'We must leave, we must leave now.'

'Why? Now that the rain has come, your grain seeds will sprout very soon. Shouldn't you stay here and take care of them?' Pele asked. He was surprised by the impatience that had come over the sisters. Yesterday they were going nowhere and they thought nothing of having been in the same place for hundreds of years. Today they wanted to leave without so much as a backward look.

'Don't worry about the grain. It will all come in its own time. We have to get to the Village of Weavers as soon as we can. Come,' Kethonuo said and hurried after her sister.

Pele was not too happy about his wet bag, which was especially heavy from all the water that had soaked into the fabric. But he followed the sisters out of their ancestral home, and they took the path that had been torn into two by the stars last night. At some places, they had to jump across the new crevices and hollows in the ground. They walked the whole day until they came to the top of a hill.

'Down there is the Village of Weavers,' Kethonuo pointed, and Pele noticed that the skin on her arm was still translucent but no longer as thin and papery as before.

The cluster of houses looked very small from the distance. They would have to walk faster in order to reach it before dark. The hills were the hunting grounds of wolves.

'Our youngest sister lives there,' Siedze said as they were going down the hill. Pele was surprised to hear that. The two women were strange enough. He wasn't sure how he would react if he met a third sister.

The descent downhill was very steep. Pele feared that if either of the women fell, they would break their bones and die there. But they were like a pair of mountain goats, easily climbing downward on their stilt legs, almost racing down the rocky slopes.

'Wait for me! Don't run, you could fall and hurt yourselves!' Pele cried out after them as he tried to keep up.

Their quickened pace brought them down the hill rather fast, and the Village of Weavers lay just a few metres from the foot of the hill.

The sisters ran ahead of Pele, heading straight for a little house of thatch that stood alone by itself. Pele followed, keeping a little distance between them and himself.

'Mesanuo!' they both called out together as they approached the house. The owner of the name opened the door immediately and they entered the house, the sisters followed by Pele.

Mesanuo looked enquiringly at Pele.

'I'm Pele. I was hosted by your sisters last night, and we have travelled together,' he said to Mesanuo as the other two made no effort to introduce him. They seemed to have forgotten all about him. They had eyes only for their sister now.

'Well?' Kethonuo asked. 'Has it happened?'

Mesanuo's face was expressionless for some moments and then she burst out, 'I'm pregnant!'

The older sisters laughed and hugged each other, and took turns to touch the rounded tummy of their sister.

Mesanuo told them how it happened: 'When I was bringing in the herbs that I had put out to dry, I heard the rain coming and before I could reach the house, a drop of rain fell on me. *A single drop of rain!* One moment the sky was overcast with angry clouds thundering and threatening, and the next moment all was clear again. The clouds passed over our village and nothing happened. Nothing except for that one drop of rain. I felt the baby grow inside as soon as that drop landed on me.'

Pele exclaimed, 'You are the woman they speak of in my village! The one whose husband and seven sons were killed by a tiger!'

Mesanuo smiled at him in confirmation of the fact. The smile lit up her face. She was transparently beautiful. Not young, just sort of ageless in a way that defied time and decay. Like her name, which meant 'the pure one', she exuded a purity of spirit that was not lost on Pele. If she was the ancient pair's sister, she must be at least two or three hundred years old, thought Pele. He smiled at how ludicrous the concept of time had become ever since he met these women.

'Come and sup with me,' she invited them all.

6

BIRTHING

Pele woke to the sounds of a baby crying softly. He turned over and tried to go back to sleep again, convinced he had been hearing things. But the unmistakable whimper of an infant came to him once more, so he sat up and peered into the dimly lit inner room. Mesanuo was holding a baby and singing to it. The child would not be soothed, and only when she suckled it did the contented sound of a hungry child that has found food replace the whimpering. Pele was astonished by it all. Yesterday she claimed that the rain had made her pregnant, and today she had birthed a child!

In a small village of the Angamis, there lived an old woman. A tiger had killed her husband and seven sons, and she spent long, lonely days waiting for the hour when she would join them in death.

One afternoon, a raindrop fell on her from the sky. She became pregnant and gave birth to a son...

That was the story that he had heard in his childhood. His grandmother had told him the story, adding that she hoped he would see it in his lifetime. But wasn't that just a story? And what was that rain yesterday that washed a whole village away but overlooked the next village, letting only a lone raindrop escape?

The world had changed ever since he met the ancient sisters. It had become a place of mystery and magic, and yet, strangely, it seemed more real than he had ever known it to be. It was as if he was emerging from a dream into some kind of truth every moment. He lay back in bed because it was still night, and he didn't know what he would say if he were to confront Mesanuo about the birthing.

He could not sleep. But he wasn't restless. As he lay there, comforted by the baby's muffled gurgling, he heard the wind building up outside. It sounded like it was whistling in the trees. But there had been no trees when they came down to the village. The valley where the Village of Weavers stood was treeless. Pele was very sure of that. So what was this sound? He didn't want to get up and investigate. Let morning come, he thought, and I will see what new wonders have been wrought in the darkness by the sisters.

Eventually dawn came flooding the valley with golden light. Pele went out of the house to look at the new phantom trees. But they were real. Young saplings that were not newly planted but had sprouted up overnight. There was no other way to describe it. They were healthy and straight and tall. Their roots were already travelling into the earth, sucking up moisture and securing a place where they had sprung up. That was not all. He walked around the village and saw that rocks and stones were standing in places where there had been none before.

Pele was not the only person walking around, marvelling at these sights. The children of the village and their parents and the headman had come out too, trying to make sense of it all.

'Is it you who has pushed a little mountain on top of our village?' the headman asked Pele. It was a good-natured question. Pele introduced himself and said that he had come in the night and knew nothing of the trees and rocks.

'It seems to be the fulfilment of an old prophecy. I hadn't imagined it would happen in my lifetime,' the headman said. 'And I must confess I didn't really believe in it. I thought it was just a story told to keep the children quiet.'

'What was the prophecy?' Pele asked.

The headman looked thoughtful, scanning the changed landscape around them. 'I've forgotten the first part, but what I remember is this: A virgin shall conceive and give birth to a son, and he will save his people. Signs and wonders shall accompany his birth, and the land shall be rejuvenated. That's all I remember. I must try to find the seer in the next village. He would know more about it. But few of us believe him.'

The headman paused. He turned to Pele, considering him with interest. 'Look at these trees, we have never had trees down here. If you don't know anything about this, there is a miracle taking place somewhere! You really don't know where the trees came from? You saw nothing last night?'

Pele shook his head. 'I went into that house as soon as I reached your village. I was with two companions and they were in a hurry to see the woman who lives there,' he pointed to Mesanuo's house.

'Ah, the tiger-widow.'

'Why do you call her that? Isn't her name Mesanuo?'

'Yes, you're right, but here everyone calls her the tiger-widow because her husband was killed by a tiger, long before any of us were born. Our elders tell us she had seven sons who went out one by one to kill the tiger but everyone was killed.'

'By the tiger?'

'Indeed it was the tiger.'

'Does anyone look after her?' Pele asked.

The headman looked away when he answered: 'No. No

one has the means to look after another person here. She lives alone and we don't know where she gets food to live on. We scarcely have enough for ourselves.'

Pele tried not to show his disapproval. What was a village that could abandon one of its own, leaving her to fend for herself?

'At least she won't be alone now,' he said. 'She gave birth to a baby last night.'

The headman's eyes nearly popped out of his head at Pele's words.

'Then it is true! The prophecy has come true!' he cried out. 'Oh God! To think that I am to see it in my lifetime!'

7

FORGIVENESS

The headman turned around and went straight to the house of the miracle birth. He would see for himself. But at the threshold he stopped and fell to his knees. He suddenly felt unworthy. What had he done in the past to take care of the tiger-widow? Very little, in fact so little that it amounted to nothing. How dare he barge in and try to partake of the miraculous birth? He looked down at his feet, and vainly tried to wipe the dust off.

The house was still as shabby as before. The roof of rusted tin was held together by old nails and rotting rafters that were sagging from the elements. The walls looked as though they would not survive a strong blast of wind, and the porch was dust covered, as though no one had lived there for years. And yet, something fundamental had changed. There was a quiet sacredness about the house. The very air felt holy, and the headman sensed that his authority had no jurisdiction over the little house of the tiger-widow. He rose, but only to stand where he was, with bowed head.

Pele saw the transformation in the confident chief of the village, who had been so garrulous when he first met him. The man looked lost and a little defeated. He could summon nothing of the knowledge he had collected in his many years as a headman to come to his aid now.

'Do you want to go inside?' Pele asked.

'I'm not worthy. I'll come later.' The headman turned around quickly and almost ran the distance to his house. Pele wondered what that was all about, but he was not surprised. This was completely out of the poor man's depth; things were happening that he could never hope to comprehend, not because they were incomprehensible, but because he was not prepared for their coming.

Pele followed him back to his house. He found the headman in his yard, washing his head and hands and collecting the water in a basin to wash his feet. When he was done, Pele asked, 'Shall we go and see the baby now?'

'Ah yes, the baby,' the headman answered, as though he had forgotten all about it. 'Yes, my son, we shall go.' He started for the door and then paused, 'Wait! I have a gift for them.'

He went in and took something from a table by the door and returned to join Pele. The two men walked back to the house of the miracle birth. Pele opened the door and made a sweeping gesture, indicating that the headman should enter.

'Widow,' the headman called out. There was no answer.

'Mesanuo,' Pele called. 'You have a visitor.'

She came out of her room carrying her child swaddled in cloth. Her face shone with happiness and it made her look beautiful.

'You are not the widow...' the headman began weakly, but he could not finish his sentence.

'Yes I am. I'm the tiger-widow. Or rather I was the tiger-widow. But I'm not that anymore. My son has changed all of that.'

Proudly she showed them the baby. Once more the headman fell to his knees, with his hands covering his face.

'Forgive us, Widow, forgive me. I didn't know, I didn't believe the stories.' He was almost weeping as he grovelled before her.

'My son forgives you, headman. Do not condemn yourself any further.'

Pele did not understand what was going on between the two of them, but he watched the exchange silently.

'Live with us here, Widow. I request you not to leave the village. Stay here as you have done and share your blessings with us as you did with our ancestors.'

'I'm no longer the tiger-widow, headman, so you can

stop calling me by that name. My son has given me the right to be called by my own name, Mesanuo.' She said it with grateful pride, and she glowed as she spoke the words.

'Stay with us, Mesanuo, even if we don't deserve your favour. Continue to make our village your home. Let your son bless us.'

'We will stay, headman. Thank you.'

The headman turned to go, but then he remembered his gift and gave it to her.

'Seed grain,' he said, pushing the small bag toward her, 'food for the future. It is for you and your son.'

Mesanuo smiled and thanked him.

The headman walked to the door but paused again, seeming to have remembered something more.

'Just one question before I go. Where have those trees and rocks come from?'

'It's called birthing, headman. The earth has birthed trees, rocks, stones, and grain, just as a mother births her offspring. The trees and rocks are the sons of the earth. Take care of them and they will take care of you and your children.'

The headman bowed low and left.

Mesanuo turned to Pele and handed him her son. Her action surprised him, but she smiled and walked out of the room.

~

Wonderingly, Pele held the raindrop son in his arms. His breath slowed down, and something shifted inside him, but it was so subtle that he hardly noticed it. Only his subconscious registered the stirring before it passed. He gazed on the pink skin of the newborn and the blue veins that ran along his cheek like the rivulets that the rain created when it ran into parched, cracked earth. The baby slept peacefully in his arms, and he recalled his mother singing a song to him when he was small.

The river runs
And it runs
Into the sea
And the sea runs
And it runs
Into the rain
Where it all comes from.

Pele sang the song softly as he carried the baby, rocking him back and forth to the rhythm of the song. The baby smiled in its sleep and the traveller continued to sing the only song he knew.

'You are a good nursemaid,' Mesanuo said when she came back and found Pele singing to her son. His voice dropped in embarrassment and though he continued singing, it was almost inaudible.

'My mother used to sing that to me,' he said by way of explanation when he stopped.

'And do you sing it to your children?' she asked.

'No. I have no children. My wife and child died in the famine.'

'I'm sorry to hear that. I know what it is to lose a loved one.' Mesanuo looked at him with sympathetic eyes.

'At least they didn't suffer like some others did.'

'Yes,' Mesanuo agreed, 'the other famine killed many more.'

'You mean the famine that took off the abandoned village?'

'No, I'm talking about the famine of stories and songs. They killed all the storytellers who tried to tell them about the Son of the Thundercloud. They killed hope.'

8

THE RIVER RUNS

'Where are your sisters?' Pele asked. He had not seen them again after the three of them reunited.

'Oh they have gone back to their house. They can't live here. They are not used to it. In any case, after the famine and the shortage of food the Village of Weavers has stopped taking in newcomers.'

'Do you think that will change? Now that your son is born?'

'I think it might,' she smiled.

'Well, they shouldn't worry about me, I may not stay long,' Pele said, though he had made no plans; he was getting used to living from one day to the next.

'It has rained in other parts, too,' he added. 'Yesterday morning, after the deluge in your sisters' village, I saw seed grain scattered here and there and lying in the crevices made by the drought. I think your sisters will not starve for long. They told me they had been eating hope for hundreds of years. *Every morning we get up and we eat hope*—Kethonuo said that to me, in exactly those words.'

'That is just like her, and that is really what they would have been doing before you came. And see how their faith has been rewarded. By the time they reach the hilltop and arrive at their home, the seed grains will not only have sprouted, but will be ready for harvest.' Mesanuo said this with great confidence.

'Why do I have no problem believing that what you say will come to pass?' Pele wondered aloud.

'Ah you are living out your name then, for your name means faith. It is actually *Kepele*, isn't it?'

Pele laughed. 'It was my grandmother's name for me. Pelevotso. My parents and friends shortened it to Pele, perhaps because it was easier to say.'

'It's a good name. I must find a name for my son too,' she said, but after some time she looked up and said, 'But he already has a name. I was told his name in my dream. How could I have forgotten it?'

Pele looked at her enquiringly. She closed her eyes and whispered, 'It is Rhalietuo. A man came to me in a dream and told me to name him Rhalietuo, because he brings the rain that will end the drought and provide food for all the villages. I shall call him Rhalie.'

She was happy to have remembered the name as it was not an ordinary name: Rhalietuo, the redeemer.

While they were talking, the headman came running to the house. 'Mesanuo, you should prepare to plant your seeds soon! Dark rain clouds are gathering; we will have plenty of rain. My wife and children are out hoeing our fields already. I shall join them too. Hurry!'

Mesanuo carried her son on her back and went out to her field. Pele followed her and took the hoe from her. 'I'll do it. I'll be quicker than you,' he said.

He was right about that, and she fed her baby and watched as Pele hoed the field, and upturned the hard soil so that the rain would run right through the earth and stay underneath, giving it the moisture it needed. It was not a thorough job, the earth was too hard for that. But he turned the soil as best he could so that the water would soak in. It had been so long since the last rain; they didn't want to waste a single drop.

Pele was turning the last furrows when the rain came. It pelted down, a great shower of water soaking them through and through. They laughed, grateful and relieved. Now the waiting was over and life could begin again.

They ran back to the house, Mesanuo holding the baby close to shield it from the rain, and Pele made a fire so they could dry their clothes. The sound of the rain was so loud, it was as though a thousand hands were throwing stones at the house. But they knew it was just rain, old rain and locked-up rain and newborn rain all falling down at the same time and making the ungodly noise that it did. It crashed down on the ground, and they almost expected to find holes in the earth when it was over. Gradually the sound diminished, although the rain never stopped falling. It simply subsided into a steady drizzle that went on through the night, like an old song that everyone knew how to hum.

The next morning, the rumbling sound of water woke Pele up. He was greatly alarmed. He ran outside to see for himself what was happening. The headman had also come out, and the village children were following behind him.

'What is that rumbling sound? Are we in danger from a rockslide here?' Pele asked anxiously.

'Not a rockslide, my son. It must be the river that used to flow below our village. That's where all the water runs to when it has rained as heavily as this. The river has been dry for so many years that we have almost forgotten its existence. Come and see!'

The small group of men, women and children wended their way out of the village and down to the riverbank. The sound of rushing waters grew louder and louder until they could no longer hear each other speak. The children had never seen a river in full spate before, and they began to cry and their mothers had to carry them back. The sight of the river was a marvelous thing. It looked so powerful as the water spewed out of its course and covered the rocks beside the river.

For now, the water threatened to overrun its banks, but eventually it would find a downward passage, and after many hours the thunderous noise would subside and become a constant low rumbling and occasional growling. The villagers would have to live with that, for this was how it was before the drought. As for the children who had never known the river, they would be taught to accept it and get used to its rough song, but also learn not to wander down to it on their own. The river was much bigger now, much more prone to flash floods and treacherous currents. Even the men would have to be very careful, and remember to respect nature the way she expected to be respected.

'The river runs!' shouted the headman when they returned to the village,

'The river runs. We are saved!'

9

OUR MOTHER

The river was once a source of life for the village. Before the drought, fathers brought home river fish and fed their families. On the river banks, the women often caught frogs that they took home to clean and dry over the wood fire, to be used as a medicinal broth when someone fell sick in the family. No one came back from the river empty-handed. There was food in the river, and so the villagers called it 'our mother'. Then the drought came. In the beginning, the river still flowed valiantly, but how long could it hold out against fate and prophecy?

The water dried down to a trickle and the villagers wept

when they saw the dying fish gasping in the sand. In the end, there were only dry-backed stones, and the children who were too young to know grew up thinking that a river was supposed to be dry and sandy and filled with rocks. 'Our mother is dead! She can no longer feed her children. Who shall be our mother when our mother is dead?' the old men and women cried and the children did not understand what they meant. Did all the old men and old women have a common mother? Were they all brothers and sisters?

But now the river was alive again and the fish leaped in the waters, and the sound of the river was a constant. The older people said to each other, 'Our mother has come back to feed us.'

'Who is that? Where is your mother?' the children asked.

'It is the name of the river. We call her our mother because she gives us food: fish, frogs, herbs and water. You must also call her by that name.'

The children laughed but they soon learned to call the river by her name.

The soil in the fields had turned soft again. The clods of earth were soaked with rainwater. It was as good a time to sow more grain seeds. The villagers went out with their seed baskets and scattered the rest of the grain in the fields. One woman came running to say, 'The ground simply swallowed up my seed making a snapping sound as though it were eating them up. It was like a live thing!'

'The soil is hungry for seed,' the headman said. 'It has

been denied seed far too long. We will have a great harvest. Let us go back and build more granaries!'

The people laughed and sang, and the oldest among them wept tears of joy.

'The prophecy said that the heavens would open and pour out rain when the Son of the Thundercloud was born. Does that mean he has been born somewhere?' the headman's wife asked.

'Yes, the prophecy is fulfilled,' her husband said. 'Come, it is time to go back.'

They followed him to the village in a long line, but not as in the past, not in despair and hopelessness, but with renewed hope, and comforted hearts.

'Follow me, all of you,' the headman said as they approached the village. He walked in through the village gate and carried on, not to his own house, but to the house of the tiger-widow.

'Why is he taking us to the tiger-widow's house?' one woman asked the headman's wife.

'How am I to know? My husband may be the headman but that doesn't mean I know everything that goes on in his head. Let us wait and see.'

A hushed silence came over the people as they assembled outside the house of the old woman they knew only as the tiger-widow. She had lived in the village longer than anyone could remember, but no one could tell exactly how old she was. No one knew when she came to the village. She had always been around, and always sadder and older than anyone else alive.

'Mesanuo! Come forth and show us the child!' the headman called.

The people heard a baby crying, and they looked at each other wordlessly. As they stood waiting and watching, the door opened slightly and a face appeared. Mesanuo opened the door further and came out carrying her son.

The women surrounded her and praised her child.

'How beautiful he is!'

'Look how black his hair is!'

'And how fair his skin!'

They asked to carry the baby and his mother graciously gave him to them. He passed from mother to mother; they handed him around, holding him very carefully, as though he were an egg. When they finally gave him back to his mother, they gazed at her in amazement. It was as if they were seeing her for the first time. Was this truly the tiger-widow? Had she not always been old? Now she looked young and beautiful, like a skywoman. If someone had come from another village and told them that a drop of rain had fallen on the tiger-widow and made her pregnant, they would have rolled on the ground laughing. But right now, nothing could stop them from believing that this graceful woman was the mother of the egg-son, the sight of whom they were filling their eyes with.

Later, when they had walked away some distance from

the tiger-widow's house, the women crowded around the headman's wife and asked her, 'What was the name your husband called her?'

'Didn't he call her Mesanuo when we were at the door?' the headman's wife asked. 'That is her name, then.'

'What happened? She used to be so old,' said one woman. 'My mother spoke of her as a very old woman! Don't you all remember, she always looked like she would die any moment. But the woman we saw back there was not old. She is not young either, but how beautiful she was, like a chief's wife, so full of dignity.'

'Remember how the tiger-widow was always so sad that you couldn't tell if she was walking bent to the ground or crawling around? This can't be the same woman,' another woman persisted.

'She is the same woman. Did you see her eyes?' the headman's wife asked. 'They are the same eyes. Only that there is life and hope where we saw grief and wretchedness before. That is the difference. The same woman looks at life differently now.'

The women marvelled at that answer, and they all had to agree that the headman's wife was right.

10

CHANGES

Prodigious activity now overtook the long period of despondency the village had known. People went to their fields and came back singing. They always found food: pumpkins and gourds from seeds that had lain in the ground during the parched years. Even the wood apple tree and the red sorrel began to bloom and bear fruit out of season. Soon there was enough grain to take in visitors and new settlers. They changed the laws on newcomers, and welcomed the ones who came to share their prosperity.

Pele had decided to stay on in the Village of Weavers. One day, standing in the fields, he wondered if he should start travelling again, but he felt no real need to. In any case, he had no destination to reach, and he didn't have much to return to. He did not feel the call of his ancestral village. He had let his past die a long time ago. He asked the headman for some land to build a house and was given a good plot of land.

Pele's house went up in a few days. It was the usual two rooms and kitchen, built from wood, bamboo and thatch with twine bindings. The mud floor was pounded down with the help of the village women who also brought cow dung that they mixed with red mud to smoothen the new floor. The smell of a new house lingered for some days, the freshly cut wood, new thatch and the pungent cow dung. It would do for a single man. He had enough space to add more rooms if he needed to.

'There is a field that belonged to my uncle. He died during the drought and there is no one in his family to till the land. You can have the field. Till it as your own,' the headman offered.

'I will pay for it.'

'No, you don't need to. I'm giving it to you free.'

'I will pay,' Pele insisted. 'In the future, when you and I are both gone, our descendants might fight over the field if it is not paid for.' So he paid for the field and went to till it the same day. It was soft, rich, loamy soil and he knew the harvest would be abundant. The water was sourced from a stream that went past his field and flowed into the other fields. There was enough water for the fields on his side of the river.

The stream was seasonal, drying up before the harvest month, but the paddy need not stand in so much water when it was about to be harvested, he reckoned.

Surprisingly the village had enough seed grain, because it was taboo to eat seed grain, even in times of famine. They also had seed grain left over from the previous years and all these were good. Pele and the villagers worked from morning till evening in their fields. After sunset, they would call to each other, 'Come, neighbour, the creator will give us another day tomorrow.' They had been away from proper field work for such a long time that it felt wonderful to be hoeing, transplanting and weeding their fields again. They had to be dragged away from it every evening with the promise that they could return the next day.

Every evening after work, Pele washed himself and went to visit Mesanuo and her son. He always took some food to them, fresh fruit and vegetables from the fields. The boy was growing rapidly. He reminded Pele of the seed grains that had fallen on the newly ploughed soil and begun to sprout instantly. Rhalie had landed on the soil of his mother's womb that had been prepared for centuries. No wonder he was like a newly sprung plant, grasping everything within reach with his tentacle hands.

'Do you have food for yourselves?' Pele asked Mesanuo one evening.

'More than enough. Look there!' she said pointing to bags of grain in the corner of the room.

'Where did you get those?' Pele asked. He had not noticed any food on the first night.

'I don't know. They were there the day I gave birth to my son.'

Pele could not understand anything about that, but he had come to expect the unusual and the miraculous wherever the raindrop son was concerned.

He lifted the boy in the air and played with him.

'Eat with us tonight,' Mesanuo offered.

'Thank you. The thought of cooking food after a hard day's work is not very tempting.'

She began to serve him food almost immediately.

'Here's some barley with *kolar* beans. Do you know that this is healthier than meat?'

Pele took the proffered plate and thanked her. She had soaked the beans overnight and cooked them close to two hours until they were tender. Bamboo shoot and a fibrous bone had been added to the beans. Pele was pleasantly surprised by the combination.

'It's very good. I can taste the richness that the beans add to the soup.'

'We've picked up many things, we who have lived longer than others on earth,' she said with a smile.

'Tell me, what was the world like before the drought?' Pele ventured to ask her.

'Not now,' she said. 'Ask me again after food.' She fed her son and made sure he was full. The little boy fell fast asleep while his mother finished eating. She placed him on the cot beside her, and washed the plates and cleared the dinner things. When she settled down by the fire, Pele looked at her and said, 'May I ask you now?'

'Of course,' she answered. 'I remember your question, Pele. I'll tell you what I know. Down here in the valley, the drought has not lasted as long as it has on the mountaintop. When I first came to live here, the earth was green and fertile. There was food everywhere. No one tilled the fields because there was no need to. We were not preoccupied with field work from dawn to dusk. And there were storytellers who went all over the land telling stories to the people, and spreading joy and hope.'

'Where are they now?'

'Dead. Killed, all killed by the dark ones, those who did not want them to transform people's minds with their stories.'

'Why?'

'Because the people sought to be free whenever they heard the stories. Free of fear, free of shame and constant desire. Without the stories, people believed they were destined to suffer, and they allowed the dark ones to enslave their minds and fill them with fear and sorrow and despair until they died.'

Pele wanted to ask a question but was silent.

'You wonder about the dark ones?' Mesanuo guessed. 'They are a group of people who have been around since before the drought. They thrive on fear and greed. They build fences, they hoard and guard, they want the trees and rivers and the stars to bend to their will. My sisters used to say they have always been here. But that is wrong. They came after the storytellers, and they let their minds grow dark and began to oppose the storytellers and the work they did.'

'Were they the ones who brought the drought?'

'No, they are powerful but not that powerful. People control their own destinies. If they choose to believe something dark, they can bring drought upon themselves. So long as the storytellers were alive, there was hope and compassion in people's hearts, and their minds received and accepted that. But when the storytellers were killed, one after the other, people slowly forgot what they had been told, or believed they were just myths, and they allowed their minds to accept the darkness. So the drought came as a result of people rejecting the joyful stories and accepting the dark stories.'

'That is incredible! If the drought was man-made, isn't there a danger that men could create another drought in the future?' Pele asked.

'There will always be that danger so long as mankind lives on earth. When people are overtaken by greed, they are going to bring a lot of trouble into their own lives and into the lives of others. Pray that this change stays. If we lose this latter rain, the world could be wiped out by a second drought.'

Her face was in darkness as she said that, but Pele saw that she looked momentarily like the tiger-widow when she pronounced the last sentence. But a few moments later when he looked at her, she was beautiful again. Pele felt his heart stir and it left him confused. He could not possibly be falling in love with her! The thought was blasphemous to him. Yet, why had he stayed on in the village? Unsettled by these revelations, he hurriedly took leave of her and went home.

11

DREAM A STRONG DREAM

'Rhalietuo!' his mother called loudly. Rhalietuo was playing with mud in the yard. It was his favourite pastime. Mesanuo smiled at his mud-caked little fingers holding clay figurines of trees, rounded blobs and more blobs that he explained were people. He placed them atop an old pot that he called a hill. Rhalietuo was four years old now. The miracle around his birth had already passed into village history and legendry, and no one asked about it anymore. When a stranger came to the village, someone would repeat the story if he asked. If not, they did not remember to say anything about it.

'My little man, you must wash your hands and come and eat food,' Mesanuo said.

'Not now, Mother. I haven't finished.'

'You can finish them tomorrow,' she said helpfully.

'Please let me do them now while the clay is still soft. If I leave it for tomorrow, the clay will go hard.'

'All right,' his mother relented, 'but don't start on another figure after you are done with that one.'

He was a typical little boy, playing all day and getting dirty or getting bruises and cuts when he ran and fell. He was allowed to play for short periods with friends of his age in the village. They were still too young and not to be trusted on their own.

'Rhalie!' his mother called again when he had not come in for quite a while. Now he came running in with water dripping from his fingers. She washed his hands again in clean water, wiped them dry, and passed his plate to him. The boy sat down and took the plate, but did not eat.

'Mother—' he started to say.

'Hush, not now. Eat first and then we will talk,' his mother answered.

Quietly he ate his food and when it was over, he turned to his mother again.

'Mother, if we plant more trees, there will be no more droughts.'

'How is that possible, my son? Do the trees hold water?'

'Trees hold hands under the earth and that is how they

hold the earth together, and they hold the water under the earth so that it stays there and doesn't go away,' the boy answered.

Mesanuo smiled at her son's logic. It was a child's reasoning and yet, why might there not be some truth in what he was saying?

'Are you going to plant mud trees?' she teased him and he laughed, filling her heart with immeasurable love.

~

They were very close, mother and son. She told him stories every night and when he fell asleep, his dreams were full of them.

One of his favourite stories was about a seed that travelled many miles to plant itself in the hand of an old man whose only daughter was dying of starvation. The father's hands suddenly filled with so much grain that it overflowed and fell to the ground. He called his wife to help him and she came running with a grain basket but it was soon full, and she had to run back and forth the whole night to empty the basket into their granary. Finally, when there was no more room in the granary, the seed shrank and became grey husk. The old man's wife ran to make a fire. She boiled the grain into porridge and served it to their daughter, and she ate and grew strong again. The old couple fed the whole village with the grain, which kept replenishing itself as soon as they had helped someone with it.

There was another story that he never tired of hearing—of the man who left his country for seven years and returned to find that his house had been occupied by a water spirit. Every night, the man waited for the spirit to fall asleep so he could steal his magic pebble from the box under his bed. But the spirit never slept. So the man sent a bee to trouble the spirit. The clever bee ran around the spirit, buzzing all the time and troubling it so much that the spirit forgot all about the house and ran out chasing the bee. The chase took them far away, at which time the man rushed in and opened the box, retrieved the magic pebble and made a net around the house so that no spirit could ever enter it again.

'If you dream of something strongly enough, your dreams will come true,' Rhalietuo's mother would tell him. He dreamt he was the seed and he dreamt he was the old man who could feed his dying daughter back to life. He dreamt he was the buzzing bee and he dreamt he was the clever man who got the better of the water spirit. He wanted to be like the old people standing on windy hilltops who could hop from hill to hill and travel the world beyond their village. He wanted to ride the wind to visit his two aunts, Kethonuo and Siedze, whom he had never met, but heard so much about.

His mother always had a story when the occasion presented itself; he could demand a story at any time and she never refused. She was a storyteller, the daughter of storytellers. But he did not know this, because she did not know this herself. Her parents had kept it a secret from her and from the world so that she would not be killed by the dark ones.

She had survived to fill his days and nights with hope and wonder. Rhalietuo dreamed of doing brave and wonderful things like the heroes in his mother's stories.

One evening, his mother told him the story of the tiger that had killed a free and fearless man and his seven sons. She never repeated the story. That night he dreamt that he had killed the tiger.

12

THE SLINGSHOT

'Rhalie!'

It was a boy's voice. Mesanuo was a little surprised to see the headman's son outside the house, calling her son. But Rhalietuo was nearly seven now, and it was only natural that he would have friends and they would come to call him out to play with them. She had been overly protective of him through his early years, never letting him play with the other boys alone, or for long. Every day mother and son went to the fields in the morning and returned after sunset, tired and happy in each other's company.

'What is his name?' she asked her son.

'Viphrü. I call him Aphrü.'

'Come in, Aphrü, Rhalie is still eating,' she called to the boy. But he refused to come into the house. 'I'll wait here,' he said kicking a stone at a bush in the yard. She tried again, but gave up. She remembered then that in the past, mothers used to stop their children from coming to her house, and wondered if something of that attitude still remained. It wouldn't surprise her.

When Rhalietuo had eaten, she instructed him, 'Greet his parents when you see them, and be careful.'

'Yes Mother,' he answered and ran off, only too happy to be allowed to play with other children. They ran to the headman's house where Viphrü produced a slingshot.

'What is that?' Rhalietuo asked.

'It's a slingshot. Have you never used one before? Here, try it.'

Rhalietuo held the y-shaped wooden handle and ran his fingers over the rubber strings that were attached to it.

'Take this,' Viphrü passed him a mud pellet. 'Put it here, hold it with your other hand and then stretch it back as far as it can go and let go. Like this!' He let go of the mud pellet and it whizzed past to smash into the stone wall a few metres away.

Rhalietuo was quite excited and he tried the slingshot, only to have it boomerang and hit him on the thumb quite hard. 'Ow!' he cried, letting go of the slingshot and putting his thumb in his mouth.

'What happened? Why did it hit my hand?' he asked.

'You were holding it too low. You are supposed to pull it up away from you like this, see?'

He tried it again and this time the pellet landed on the grass harmlessly. He ran to pick up the undamaged pellet and shot it again, thrilled when it smashed into the stone wall.

Pele was in the house with the headman when the boys were playing. He came out to watch and told Rhalietuo that he would make him a slingshot if he wanted.

'Can you make it today, Anie Pele?' asked the boy excitedly. Pele said he could because there wasn't much to it, except to get a strong y-shaped twig and rubber string and an old piece of leather for the projectile. Pele found all these items in the headman's house and went to work on the slingshot. When it was finished and Pele handed it over to him, Rhalietuo's joy knew no bounds.

'Careful you don't use it to shoot the chickens,' Pele warned.

Pele watched Rhalietuo and Viphrü as they played together. Boys will be boys, he thought.

Soon enough the boys were squabbling over the mud pellets and over how many Rhalietuo had already shot. Viphrü was the youngest in his family, and used to always getting his way. He didn't like that his friend was not willing to give back his mud pellets. He began to hit Rhalie with the slingshot. Before Pele could pull them apart, Viphrü had landed a hard knock on Rhalie's nose and it started to bleed. Both boys were crying loudly, Rhalie in Pele's arms and Viphrü behind his mother's skirt.

'What happened? I thought you were playing together nicely,' she asked.

'He took all my pellets,' Viphrü sniffled.

'That's not true,' Rhalie protested, 'he gave me some himself.'

The grownups took over and Pele said he would take the boy with the bloodied nose home. When they arrived at Rhalie's house his mother was appalled to see him bleeding.

'Rhalie! Did you fall and hurt yourself?' Mesanuo was very upset, and even more upset when she heard what had happened. She washed her child's face with cold water and made him lie with his head on her lap. Slowly the nose bleed stopped.

'I don't want you to play with him again, Rhalietuo, ever,' Mesanuo said.

Pele wanted to tell her not to be so careful with the boy. It was inevitable that he would get into scrapes with the others. She would just have to accept it; she couldn't keep him tied to her all the time. She shouldn't impose her isolation on the boy.

But he wasn't sure he knew her well enough to risk telling her that. Watching her caress the boy's forehead, oblivious to all the world, he felt like an intruder. Then he noticed that she was crying silently, as if her heart had been broken. Confused, and unaccountably sad, he turned and walked out of the house.

13

SISTERS

'I've been dreaming of them for several nights. I want to take Rhalietuo to meet them before anything happens to them,' Mesanuo confided in Pele one day.

She was talking about her sisters, whom she had not seen since the night her son was born.

'They said they would come back, but they haven't. I worry about them. At least Rhalietuo is big enough now to walk halfway on his own. I couldn't have managed earlier if I had to carry him all the way. I can visit them now.'

'May I come with you?' Pele asked.

'Why?'

'I'd like to see them again too. If not for them, maybe I wouldn't have come here.'

'Come then. We'll get ready today and leave at dawn tomorrow.' Pele was a bit surprised at the plan but he knew better than to question her. He would let the headman know of his intention and accompany them. He packed things he felt they would need on a long journey, and threw in some basic carpentry tools.

When morning came, the sky was overcast. Pele got up and took his bag and went to Mesanuo's house. The door was open so he went in.

'Mesanuo, it looks like it's going to rain. Should we postpone the trip?'

'No, we have to leave now. There should be no further delay. The rain will not stop us. The sooner we leave the better.'

She had a small bag and so had her son. She locked the door to the house and pulled a sack of grain over the doorway.

'What is that for?' Pele asked, gesturing at the sack of grain.

'It means any stranger who needs food may help himself to the grain. I don't know how long we'll be away, and it is a sign of hospitality to guests even if I'm not around to host them. Now that we have food, we should not hoard it for ourselves, lest we lose it all again.'

Only a woman would be capable of such sensitivity, Pele

thought. And among women, too, only a few. It was a good world that had women like Mesanuo and her sisters. And suddenly he had a vision of his grandmother in her remote hut, where the animals came to be healed. He had seen it only once. Perhaps he should go there some day, though it had probably disappeared now, claimed by the forest.

~

The path they took was dark and difficult. It was uphill all the way.

They had been climbing for an hour when it began to rain heavily, drenching them to the skin.

'Shouldn't we stop and rest somewhere?' Pele asked.

'No, this will not last long, but if we stop we will never reach our destination.'

Pele found that hard to understand but did not want to argue with her. They plodded on, with the rain pounding at them, and making visibility difficult. The force of the rain became so great that it slapped at their skin through their clothing. It was like a living thing, the rain. Unable to see straight ahead of them, they walked with heads down, but the rain battered them sideways so that they felt that they were walking into a wall of water. There was something unnatural about the rain, the way it surrounded and intimidated them. It was almost as though it was trying to obstruct their journey. Mesanuo took the lead and went on. She was hard as iron, unswerving in the face of the dark and angry downpour. When they reached a curve in the path, and managed to climb up one of the peaks, the rain suddenly stopped.

The land before them was completely dry.

'What was that?' Pele had to ask. 'Where did that rain go? How is it possible?'

Mesanuo looked back and said, 'That was not rain. It was a spirit sent to stop our journey, which was why it was so important to continue climbing.' She opened her cloth to show him her arms. 'Look.' There were little cuts all along her arms, and beads of blood.

'Mother! You've hurt yourself!' Rhalie cried.

'Don't worry, son. It's over now.'

She found some medicinal herbs and made a paste and rubbed it on the cuts. The bleeding stopped and she pulled her cloth over her arms again.

'Let me carry your bag,' Pele offered.

She handed it over without any protest. She lifted her son on her back and they continued uphill.

'My son does not fear the rainstorm. He sees his father in it,' she said. And Pele remembered that Rhalie had not cried even once during the terrible storm.

'He's not the raindrop son for nothing, is he?' he laughed.

They continued climbing, but there were no obstacles now, and though the way ahead was steep it was straightforward. Pele recollected that when he was running down this path years ago with the two sisters, the trees were dead, and many trees were lying with roots upturned. But now he could see only young green trees everywhere. It was as though a giant hand had removed the dead trees and planted new ones all over the hill. The rocks were still there beside the path, but they were moss-covered now. The change was so complete that Pele could not believe he was going back on the same path.

It was a demanding trek, uphill all the way, but by afternoon they had reached the top and begun their descent. They could see the abandoned village in the distance, but they would need to walk hours before reaching it. Still, the sight of the village warmed their hearts. It was too far to make out anything; they couldn't, for instance, see signs of human habitation yet. But the house was standing. That in itself was a good sign.

The three travellers continued their journey, passing more forests of trees until the last bit of steepness eased off and the ground was plain from then on. The moss underneath blessed their tired feet, and they sank their feet gratefully into its softness. The tree line should have stopped below the upper path, but they still found trees on the top of the hill. The growth was thinner of course, but the fruit on the branches testified to the fact that birds and smaller animals dwelt here in safety.

Finally, they saw the house close by.

It stood quite alone, its neighbours having all been taken

off by the rainstorm. All around the house grew grain, in different stages of ripeness. There was no evidence that anyone had ploughed the ground there, yet the grain was full husked and healthy. There was a wisp of smoke rising lazily above the chimney. Mesanuo's heart warmed to see that sign, and tears came easily to her.

'They are alive. They are there. See the smoke?' she turned gratefully to Pele.

'Come Rhalie, you will meet your aunts.'

14

REUNION

The travellers quickened their pace. Both Kethonuo and Siedze stood outside at the doorway, ready to welcome their visitors.

'You knew we were coming?' Mesanuo asked excitedly.

'Someone had a dream,' Kethonuo said with a mischievous glint in her eyes. 'But let her tell you herself. I am not the owner of the dream.'

Siedze smiled at Kethonuo's words, but said nothing. Instead she held out her hands to Rhalie and said, 'Welcome to our home, nephew.'

Rhalie showed no fear of his aunts and he wandered all over the house, examining everything in it curiously.

Pele was surprised to see that the roof he had covered with the old tarpaulin and jute was still in place. He could see all the openings in the roof through which he had watched the stars. He looked at the spot where he had lain the last time and smiled. Nothing had changed.

Pele had expected the sisters to look different from the last time he had seen them. After all, they had food in abundance now. But even they appeared unchanged. The only different thing about them was that they were calm and carefree, if that adjective could be applied to them. The constant air of waiting that had defined their very existence was gone. 'Forgive me,' he said, 'but I must ask. How have you lived all these years? Your village is no longer as it was before, yet you are both as I remember you from that evening I first met you.'

Kethanuo answered him: 'We told you we lived on hope. Now our hope has come to fulfilment. Did you see the stalks of grain around the house? We have no dearth of food now. No need to plough and toil in the fields. The fields have come to our door, saying, "Harvest us, eat us, so we can grow up again." And that is what we keep doing whenever we need food. But as for our spirits, we are fulfilled. We are ready to go anytime now.'

Mesanuo was shocked at that announcement.

'No! I can't bear to be alone here.'

'You are not alone, sister. You have a son to look after.'

Mesanuo looked over at her son, and the smile came

back to her face. Kethonuo noticed this and asked, 'Do you want to hear Siedze's dream now?'

Siedze began, without waiting for their response: 'I dreamed that I had travelled down to the valley where Mesanuo and her son live. The village was full of warriors. They carried tall spears with sharpened tips that glinted in the sun. Some of the spears were decorated with red goats' hair and others with carvings, and some spears were double-pronged. I watched from afar as the warriors shook their spears in the sunlight and ululated war cries, and made every heart watching them tremble. They were going to hunt the tiger, they said, and the army of warriors marched forth from the village.

'As they went out, their marching sounded like thunder on the hilltops, and my heart trembled for them. Soon I heard cries of men, terrible cries of death and destruction. I ran to the peak to see what was happening. It was the warrior army. They had gone to attack the tiger, but one by one they were all killed by the tiger, and none of them returned.

'I cried and cried when I saw that. I asked "Who shall kill the tiger now?" And as I watched, a little boy marched in, dressed like a warrior. He had a shield, and a spear, but he was too small and I feared for his life. But he was fearless and when the tiger roared, he threw his spear into the tiger's mouth. It went right inside and pierced the tiger's heart and the beast finally died!'

Siedze was so excited by her dream that she was clapping when she finished her narrative.

'But what is the meaning of your dream, sister?' Mesanuo asked.

It was Kethonuo who replied: 'It is simply this. There will be many warriors who will try to kill the tiger. They will all die because they will make the mistake of trying to kill the tiger with pride. The warriors lifting their spears and ululating means they are putting their trust in their spears and their own strength. The tiger is a spirit tiger; he is no ordinary being. You cannot kill a spirit tiger with worldly weapons. The best, well-tempered spear is no match for a spirit tiger. The boy, on the other hand, had no pride. He was not fighting to earn a name for himself as the others were doing. He wanted to kill the tiger to stop it from hurting any more people. The boy's heart was pure; do you see?'

'That's a wonderful dream!' Pele exclaimed.

'It is a good dream, especially since I have dreamed it just before your coming,' Siedze said.

The adults knew what she was alluding to, but they did not say anything more in front of the boy. Words were so important. The wrong words pronounced over a person would destroy him. The right words spoken judiciously would lead a person to fulfil his destiny.

'Come and eat what we have.' Kethonuo led them into the kitchen where there were pots with warm food. They ate heartily and Rhalie was soon fast asleep. The others sat around the fire and talked. Pele told them about life in the village, and all about the river that was providing food again now. Mesanuo mentioned the incident of the fight between Rhalie and the headman's son.

'Such incidents will increase, sister. Your son will be envied by people. Even if they see the goodness of his heart, it will only cause greater envy. Many will admire him, but they will fail to love him. Others will resent him for his goodness. It has always been this way. It is the dark side of humanity.'

'Must we continue living there? Can't we move here and live with you?'

'Are you trying to stop the prophecy from being fulfilled?' Kethonuo looked very severe. She tilted her head at the sleeping form of the boy. 'If he is the one chosen to kill the tiger, would you prevent him from fulfilling his destiny?'

'I have spoken without wisdom, sister. Forgive me,' Mesanuo replied.

Pele was a silent observer throughout this conversation. He struggled to understand the drift of it all. Some things were clear—the boy Rhalietuo had a great destiny before him. He would kill the tiger and avenge his father and brothers. But the sisters had denied Mesanuo the opportunity to move here and live with them. He had to trust that they knew what they were saying. They were not ordinary people; he was quite sure of that. Their lives were to be lived heroically or not at all, no matter how hard that was.

He looked from one sister to the other in the dim light of the fire. While Mesanuo looked more youthful than ever, her older sisters were the opposite. They had not grown any healthier than before, and yet they had not grown any older than he remembered. They had been eating well and certainly had enough food. But it was not that. It was nothing physical, or tangible. It was as though they were past the nourishment that earthly food could provide. Even as Mesanuo was taking in more of the earth, the other two were growing more detached from the needs of the flesh. It was as though they had begun to transcend the mortal. Mesanuo must have feared that this was happening, and so she must have insisted on making the journey without delay. After all, she was one with them, he thought.

Sisters. How strange. No other members of a family could be more different from one another as the three of them were. One was regenerated and reborn while the other two were so clearly pulling away from earthly life that it came as a surprise that they were still there in flesh and blood.

'This will also be your last visit,' Siedze said unexpectedly, breaking the silence.

'But you may stay as long as you want,' Kethonuo interrupted. 'Don't think of yourselves as guests. You may stay here for as long as you can, if your fields will not suffer from your absence.'

'Of course,' Siedze joined in, 'we only wanted to prepare you, sister, for a parting that is inevitable. But you won't stay behind for too long. The sooner we go, the sooner you can join us. That is the way it is.'

At first, Mesanuo looked stricken at the news, but she calmed herself and said, 'May it be as you say.'

'Your youth has been renewed for a purpose. Rhalietuo needs a young, strong mother, someone to be both mother and father to him. One day he will no longer need you. One day it is he who will take care of you,' Siedze said. Then she added, 'In this world or another.'

15

OUT OF THE CHASM

In the morning, Rhalie was up before anyone else. Excitedly he called his mother and asked if he could go out and explore. The little boy's whispered pleas woke up Pele, who took some time to recall where he was.

'You mustn't go out alone. Wait, I will come with you,' his mother said, getting up and covering herself with her body cloth. *The chasm*! Mesanuo wouldn't know about the chasm outside the house! Pele hurriedly got up and ran after them.

'Wait! Be careful where you are going!' he shouted. Mesanuo and Rhalie stopped in their tracks, and waited for him to catch up with them.

They were inches from the chasm and had Pele not shouted, their next step would have flung them headlong into it. Mesanuo saw the danger for the first time, and with a little cry she pulled her son to her. But the ground was slippery from the rain, and they were both slithering towards the mouth of the chasm. Pele ran to them and pulled them back until they found a safe place to stand some distance away. Recovering themselves, they looked downward. The chasm made by the stars was overgrown with bushes and small plants. It looked like a little wild garden now, no longer as threatening and as dreadful as when Pele had first seen it. Nevertheless, if they had fallen in, they would have broken an ankle on the rocks hidden beneath the shrubbery and vegetation.

'What is it? I have never seen this before!' Mesanuo gasped.

'It was made by the stars the night before I came to your village. I was lying in your sisters' house watching the open skies when I saw the stars move and pull the earth with them. In the morning when we came out of the house, this chasm was there. It was much more dangerous back then. The ground gaped open and there were sharp rocks down there that would have killed anyone who fell into the chasm.'

'The stars pulling the earth? Hmm, how long have you known my sisters?'

'I was their guest only for that one afternoon and night.

I slept on the floor because there were no beds in the house. I saw the stars move in the skies, and I felt the earth move beneath me every time the stars pulled it. In the morning, it rained so heavily we feared we would be taken off by the rain. Whatever remained of the old houses was washed away, all except your sisters' home, and the surplus water ran into the chasm, so the chasm was a blessing in disguise.'

'That sounds like a dream, but I know you have to be telling the truth,' Mesanuo said.

'The stars must have changed the course of the river below your village. The headman said that the river had dried up for many years.'

'That's quite possible. But that would not be the only reason for the stars pulling the earth eastward. That was the day my son was born. That was a sign too,' she said simply.

'Quite likely,' Pele agreed. 'After all, it's not only the changing of river courses that the stars are interested in.' He smiled as he said this.

Rhalie had found some berries and was absorbed in plucking them while the two adults stood nearby talking.

'I'm sorry if this visit has been painful for you,' Pele began. 'I know how much you were looking forward to it.'

'The pain is not important. It's part of the physical that I must learn not to embrace. Remember how hard it rained when we were coming up here? Something did not want us to come here. Something tried to stop us getting to see my sisters and learning from them. I'm convinced that my son has a great destiny to fulfil, but now I know I am part of it, and I must strengthen my heart so that he can live out that purpose.'

'Did you mean the killing of the tiger?' Pele asked.

'Yes, but that is much bigger than we think we know. I don't think my sisters know all about it either.'

'Nobody does. Life is unknowable.'

'I don't agree, Pele. Life is hard and unexpected, but we can direct it to go the way we want it to. It is up to us.' Her answer surprised him. The soft and vulnerable woman he thought he knew down in the valley had become a different person up on the mountaintop. He tried to define her, and groped for words. She had grown stronger. Could it be the meeting with her sisters that had done it? Maybe it had started from the time they encountered the vicious attack by the rain? No, she hadn't actually grown hard; she simply appeared more certain.

'Mother!' Rhalie called, 'I've collected so many berries, look!' His little hands were full of wild raspberries. His shirt was stained with berry juice because he had been eating the berries and dribbling the juice down his shirt front.

'Will you have some, Anie Pele?' he came forward with his offering.

'Thank you.' Pele took a couple of berries and said, 'Let's go back and get you cleaned up.' He picked up the boy and the three of them returned to the house.

There was food cooked and waiting for them. Kethonuo

served them and said apologetically, 'We don't eat meat.' But the food she made was very tasty. It was a broth of fresh herbs and dried herbs seasoned with *khuvie*, the country chives that were abundant in these parts.

'It's not possible to miss meat when you are eating such splendid food,' Pele remarked.

'We use mushrooms as meat supplements and find it much healthier,' Kethonuo replied. 'Siedze is the mushroom gatherer. She finds them in the woods and dries them, so we always have a good supply.'

All of them ate well. The conversation in the house was much lighter today, and Pele noticed that the sisters were trying to entertain their young guest with different items. He had found a spool of very old yarn. Siedze laughed as she showed him the circular wooden spindle that had been used to hold the yarn. She began to demonstrate how to use the spindle. He was preoccupied with it for a long time.

They then took their visitors on a little tour outside the house. Pele could not believe his eyes. The landscape was completely transformed. The crater-like holes in the ground that he had seen when he first came had disappeared. In their place stood verdant vegetation, most of it edible herbs and shrubs.

'What about the wolves? Do they come near?' he asked the sisters.

'We haven't seen or heard them since the rainstorm.'

'Could the rain have taken them?' he laughed.

'We're not sure. That old rain could have done anything it wanted, you know.' Kethonuo's eyes gleamed in merriment.

They headed back to the house and Pele pointed out a spot. 'Look Mesanuo, this is where Siedze was lying on the floor saying she wanted to look at the rain. I thought she was totally crazy. I had just repaired the roof and hoped it would shelter us sufficiently, but she was least bothered. She only wanted to look at the rain!' Pele pointed to the spot on the ground where Siedze had pulled her mat and then lain down to watch the rain because she had never seen it in her life.

'And you? Where were you, Anie Pele?' Rhalie asked him.

'I lay here,' Pele pointed to the other side of the floor, 'underneath the newly patched roof. But I lay on my back because I wanted to watch the stars pull the earth.'

They all laughed at the memory of that night. It was a little hard to believe that seven years had passed since then, and so little had changed. But that was not true; things had changed. Minds and hearts had changed, and grown to accept a reality that was much larger than any of them could comprehend. It was as though they had all climbed out of a chasm, and begun to see the real purpose of their lives.

'I actually feel…reborn—if I may use such a term. Things that I learned as I was growing up no longer fit or belong, and this is the only reality I want to hold on to,' Pele said with some difficulty as he tried to put into words how he felt. He tried, but he felt deeply inadequate.

16

SIEDZE

Siedze and the boy were inseparable. She was never too tired to play with him. She took him to gather mushrooms and taught him how to find the fungus growing beneath rocks or in damp places. The others heard cries of delight whenever he found a new grove of mushrooms. Siedze would inspect his find carefully, and permit him to gather only if they were edible, and, just as importantly, mature enough. If they were not mature, she would not allow him to harvest them. Rhalie was an obedient boy, and he was a quick learner. His aunt rewarded his efforts by making him marvellous broths of mushrooms and fresh herbs for supper. He was thrilled when his mother told him that he had provided food for the family with his find.

There were berries too, and the pair were never too tired to go berry picking. Besides the wild raspberries, there were orange coloured cape gooseberries in their gossamer coverings, and land berries that were purple and round and had a bitter aftertaste. Rhalie did not care for those, but Siedze said they were very good for a tummy ache.

Every morning they disappeared for an hour or two before reappearing with their harvests of herbs, berries and mushrooms. They found birds' nests and she showed him an owl's sitting place, promising they would stay up at night and listen to it hoot. But every evening after dinner, he would fall fast asleep on his mother's lap, and wake up disappointed in the morning when he remembered what he had missed.

One morning they were out as usual, looking for berries and food from the wild.

'What amazing hands you have, Azuo Siedze!' Rhalie remarked. Immediately she hid her hands behind her back and was a little offended. She felt deeply self-conscious and slightly insulted that a mere boy should throw such a casual comment at her.

'What about them, boy?' she asked sternly.

Rhalie thought she was teasing him, and ran behind her to pull out her hands. But she was in earnest and refused to let him see them. No matter how hard he pulled and asked, she adamantly refused to show her hands.

'What's wrong with my hands, boy?' she snarled at him.

'Wrong? Nothing's wrong with them. They are so strong. I wonder how you got so strong. I want to be strong in my hands like you, Azuo Siedze,' he replied.

A little ashamed, she dropped her hands and hesitantly held them out to him. She turned the sinewy and leathery side downward and opened her palms. The boy buried his face in them and inhaled deeply. 'I just love your hands,' he whispered, and she, she who had never heard anyone say that to her, shut her eyes fast, but not quick enough. A large tear squeezed its way out and landed in the boy's hair.

He kept his eyes shut and held on to her hands. 'I think it's going to rain,' he said with eyes closed.

'Not right now, but maybe a bit later,' she said. 'We can stay here for some time.'

They sank down on the grass, the boy's face still buried in Siedze's hands and his nose pushed into her palm; they stayed that way for a long time.

Siedze could not understand why Rhalie loved her hands. To her, they were ugly, with their spidery veins becoming more and more visible every day. The skin stretched over her bones and veins was just a veneer now, an excuse to claim that she was human. It bound her and Kethonuo to the earth. But lately they had both been waking up with the knowledge that it was just by a hair's breadth that they were here on earth.

'I can't feel my legs anymore!' Kethonuo had exclaimed

one morning. Siedze had quickly gotten up to examine, but she'd had to cover her mouth so as not to scream at what she saw.

'What is it?' Kethonuo had asked. 'Why are you so alarmed?'

'Your legs, they are not there!'

'What do you mean?' Kethonuo had struggled to get up and look, but she had fallen back again.

'I have no legs? What can you see, Siedze? Please tell me.'

Siedze had taken a deep breath and looked again. The outline of her sister's legs and feet had then slowly begun to reappear and they were restored to their owner. But just before that, she had seen her sister transforming into spirit, flesh and bone disappearing and essence taking their place. There wasn't much time left at all.

Siedze looked down at the boy's head in her hands now. She felt a bittersweet pang in her heart. To know love now when it was so near departure! She would be wise. She would take the sweetness and let the bitterness be. She had never been loved like this before. She didn't mean there had been no family love, that had been there, always there, but to be loved by another person, an outsider, who could surely see your flaws—someone who loved you, simply, for yourself! It was so wondrous, and she allowed the glow of that love to linger a little longer.

She stole a glance at her hands. They were still the same, the spidery veins pulsating beneath blue skin cover. But no, they were no longer the same; they were loved, they were transformed, and for the first time in her long life she saw her hands as beautiful. That was enough for her, for now. That would do.

'Shall we go back home, little one?' she asked gently.

'Oh I was almost falling asleep. I felt so safe when you were holding me, Azuo Siedze.'

They had not gathered enough berries, but her heart was full and could hold no more. 'We can come out again later,' she promised. 'Let's go back so your mother doesn't miss you.'

17

A HOUSE FOR PELE

In later years Pele was never sure how long they had all stayed together in the abandoned village. After some time, he went to the forest and cut wood and repaired the house as well as he could, dismantling the old, rotten beams and replacing them with new ones. There was no tin available, so he made a plaited roof of cane over the house, laid thin lines of wood over it and covered it with layers of elephant grass. It took him many days to complete it, but at the end he had managed to build an extra room for Mesanuo and Rhalie, and low beds for them all.

Pele chose to walk long distances into the woods to

collect material for the house, taking care not to cut too many trees in the same area. His reason for going far from the mountaintop was that he did not wish to disturb the fragile ecology around the abandoned village site. The vegetation was new and young, and he feared that any sudden disturbance of that newly found balance would cause greater damage than could be repaired. So, he walked as far as he could from the abandoned village, well below the tree line, and carried back the logs he would use on the house. He used native oak and eucalyptus, because it withstood sun and rain better than other wood. Rhalie wanted to accompany him on these trips, but Pele worried that the boy would not be able to walk the whole route, and then he would have to carry him, and lose a perfectly good work day. Sometimes he allowed Rhalie to come if his mother could accompany them on the trip. Together they chose good trees and marked them. If he could not carry back all the wood in one trip, he would leave some behind for the next day.

'Why are you doing this?' Mesanuo had asked in the beginning. Strangely, even Pele could not explain why he was putting so much time and effort into this project.

'My spirit tells me it is important and worthwhile. I don't know beyond that. Someday when it becomes clearer to me, I will tell you more.'

'It is a good thing,' she said. 'See how happy they are. For the first time, they have a real home to live in.'

'And they have a real family to share it with. They love having you and your son with them.'

'And they love having *you* around too. They almost seem to know you better than I do.' Mesanuo laughed as she said this. It was true. Though the sisters and Pele had spent just twenty-four hours together before they travelled to Mesanuo's home, they were now like old friends. It amused Mesanuo that her sisters fussed over Pele and offered him generous portions of food whenever it was mealtime.

'They are wonderful beings, both of them. I've never met anyone as wise as them,' Pele said, his words light with frank affection.

'So true,' Mesanuo agreed. 'I used to fear them when I was growing up, until I found out that they loved me dearly. They seemed so stern before but now they are like children, laughing and enjoying the simplest of things. Did you see yesterday how Kethonuo was juggling two pears to entertain Rhalietuo?'

'Yes, they would do anything for that boy. I've seen Siedze looking very impatient to take him out in the morning. It's become their morning ritual, and I suspect neither of them would miss it for anything.'

'I'm so happy here, Pele. I can even forget what life has been like in the Village of Weavers, and pretend I never lived there.'

Her words surprised Pele. He looked at her questioningly. 'I thought you liked it there. You've been living there for so long.'

'I had no choice. I had nowhere to go after I lost them all; I could not. My husband was headman of the village. We lost a few people to the tiger that summer. My husband went out to kill the tiger and was killed instead. My sons were young, but as soon as they grew older they wanted to kill the tiger. One by one they went out, and all of them were killed by the tiger. Each time, it was a sharp knife thrust in an unhealed wound in my heart. When my last son died, the village turned against me. You've heard them call me the tiger-widow?'

'Yes, I heard them say that in the first days.'

'There were two women who said that it was my spirit, and not the tiger, that had killed all my sons and my husband. The village refused to have anything to do with me after that. Their children were warned not to come to my house and I was isolated from the village, even while living within it. I was never allowed to take part in the festivals.'

'That is inhuman. It was not your fault that the tiger killed their family members or yours.'

'No. But sometimes people think that repeated tragedies have a source in the family itself. Mine has been a very lonely life before Rhalietuo was born.'

'Why didn't you leave?'

'My life is not confined to the life I live within the village, Pele. I knew that part of fulfilling the prophecy was staying on in the village, enduring the isolation and making myself obedient.'

'I'm so sorry for all the pain you have endured,' Pele said with sincerity.

'It's over now. You brought the rain and see what it has brought me,' she said pointing to her son. He simply smiled back without saying anything.

~

That evening, when they had finished eating, Pele asked if he might make a small shed for himself in a corner of their land.

'There is no need for you to ask our permission. You are as much an owner as us,' Kethonuo said.

'No, that isn't true. This has been your village for four hundred years. I'm an outsider who never knew there was a village here until the day we met. Of course I should ask permission, and you may grant it.'

'Why do you need to build a house?' she asked.

'Why do people build a house? To live in it? Or to keep it standing for spirits to live in?' he teased her.

The sisters looked at each other wide-eyed and clapped for joy.

They quickly agreed that Kethonuo would point out an area for Pele to build a house, and they did this as soon as it was morning. She used her stick to demarcate a wide area of land on which he could build a house and keep a garden. She made sure it was close enough to their house.

Pele didn't take many weeks to build the two-room

shed. It was enough for one person and he would live there comfortably enough, eating his meals with the sisters and sleeping under his own roof. The day after it was built, Rhalietuo came to him.

'Anie Pele, can you help me build my own house?'

'Certainly, my small man. We can start today.'

The two of them went into the forest and brought back short logs and bamboos, and built a little shed for the boy. Rhalie was thrilled beyond measure! He insisted on sleeping in his own house at night, but he wanted his mother with him.

'Mother, please, it will be just one night, please.' Mesanuo could not possibly refuse such a request, so they made a soft bed out of grass and pulled their mats over the grass. When it got dark, they crawled into the hut and lay under the stars.

'I can see all the stars, Mother!' he said excitedly.

'Not all, my son. There are more stars than these, but we cannot see them because they are on the other side of the sky,' his mother replied.

'Can we go there someday?'

'I'm sure we could if we really want to. I'm sure nzuo Kethonuo and nzuo Siedze know all about it. You can ask them.'

Rhalie was so excited he could not sleep. Everything was new and exhilarating for him. That night the moon was a dark circle with a white ring around it. He wanted to know if the wolves had eaten up the inside of the moon.

18

PARTINGS

In order to keep track of the days and weeks, Pele made a notch on a beam for every passing week. Life in the abandoned village was good. There was plenty of food, and the sisters led peaceful lives.

Rhalie had no friends of his age, it was true, but when they remembered the headman's son hitting him on the nose and making him bleed, they felt that he did not lack for anything up here. His aunts and mother and Pele were the best friends he could ever have.

In a year's time the boy had learned to gather edible berries and detect which mushrooms were poisonous and which were full of nutrition. He still managed to bring home herbs that had to be thrown out, but he was slowly learning the names of the herbs and their habitat. It was the best education anyone could have. And the boy was growing. He reached up to Pele's chest at the end of the fourth year.

'Azuo Kethonuo, I'm going to be a carpenter when I grow up!' he announced proudly one day.

'Well, that is wonderful! But why a carpenter? Why would you choose to be a carpenter?' she asked.

'Because houses are important. If we didn't have houses we would have to sleep outdoors in the rain and cold. Anie Pele said he will teach me to make houses.'

'I see. That is an excellent thing. Will you make me a house then?'

'I will, but first I will make myself a bigger house, because my house is getting too small for me. When I stand up, I keep hitting my head on the ceiling.'

Pele laughed and said he would offer his help to do that. And soon they had made the little house bigger and lifted the roof a good deal higher. Rhalie began to bring a portion of the food he had gathered and arranged it in neat rows in a corner of his house.

'Mother, this is my kitchen,' he explained one day. 'It's the same as Azuo Siedze's and Azuo Kethonuo's.' The sisters admired his work, and no one laughed at him.

'I love it here, Mother, can we always stay here?' he asked another day. Mesanuo held him close to her and said, 'We'll try to stay as long as we can. But we will have to go back to the Village of Weavers one day.'

'But why? I like it here; I don't like it down there.'

'Yes, but my dear, you must see that nzuo Kethonuo and nzuo Siedze will not be with us forever. When they are gone, we'll have to go back home.'

Rhalie was not happy about it at all, and that night at dinner he was very quiet. After eating he went and sat beside Kethonuo with a serious look on his face.

'Azuo Kethonuo, Mother says that when you are gone, we have to go back to the Village of Weavers. May I not stay here in my little house?'

Kethonuo looked from one adult to the other, and then she said very carefully, 'This is not a village, Rhalietuo. This village has no name. In fact, you have heard us call it the abandoned village. It is taboo to live in an abandoned village. For now, it may seem as though everything is nice here: we have plenty of food, we have trees and fruits and mushrooms, and we have each other. But an abandoned village is abandoned for a reason, so that people do not live in it again.'

'There is another thing about life,' Kethonuo continued. 'People grow up and grow old and die so that new people can take their place. And before they die, they are meant to do some things. That is the reason why we are here in the first place.'

'I don't want you to grow old and die,' Rhalie said with a little catch in his voice.

Kethonuo paused before speaking.

'We are very old already. Look at us, my dear child, I am more than four hundred years old, and nzuo Siedze is more than three hundred and eighty-five years. If we don't die, we will suffer so much because we will not be able to eat, or run, or sleep, or breathe. It is a good thing that we are made to die. You wouldn't want us to suffer just because you don't want us to die, would you?'

With a pained face, he answered, 'No, I wouldn't want you to suffer, but I wouldn't want you to die either.'

'That is called love, my dear. When we love someone, we don't want to let them die, but when we love them very much, we don't want them to suffer.'

'Well then, I hope I will die soon after all of you are dead,' the boy said, finding his own simple solution to life's hardest question.

'I'll tell you something: death is not forever. But do you know what is forever?' Kethonuo asked.

'No, tell me.'

'Love is forever. If you love us, your love is stronger than death and even death cannot separate us.'

'I love you, I love all three of you, all four,' he said, stretching his arms out wide.

~

One morning, Kethonuo took Mesanuo aside and told her that they must prepare to leave the next day. Mesanuo was very sad, but she knew that it was inevitable.

'The sadness will pass, because each day of your life will bring you closer to meeting us again,' Kethonuo said to her youngest sister. Mesanuo wiped her tears and went to tell Pele what her sisters had said.

'Can we stay one more day?' Pele asked.

'No. When they say that we should leave tomorrow, we should not disobey them. It is for our safety, and for Rhalie's.'

'I'll get ready. Are you going to tell him? I guess you had better.'

There were no questions from Rhalie that night. Dinner was a quiet affair, with everyone preoccupied with his or her own thoughts. Now and again Mesanuo let out a heavy sigh, and then she regretted it and tried to cover up.

When morning came, the sisters were impatient for the visitors to depart.

'Here, don't forget this,' Siedze said, passing packets of food to them. She had also packed seed-grain for them, and made sure they had everything they needed. She refrained from embracing Rhalie, but she laid her hand on his head, and for the last time, covered his face with her hands and stayed like that for minutes. He wouldn't look at her until the very last moment.

Kethonuo said goodbye from her bed. That was a little strange, thought Pele, that she did not get up to bid them farewell. He stepped back to look at her and she hurriedly pulled her mat up to cover herself. But in the instant it took her to do that, he saw that the lower part of her body was already metamorphosing into spirit. Half of her was gone. The realization stiffened Pele in his tracks and he lifted his hand to say goodbye but stopped short of touching her.

'Come,' he pleaded with Mesanuo at the door, 'We must leave now if we don't want to be caught in the woods in the dark.' It was a good excuse to drag her away. One last goodbye wave to Siedze and they were on their way. When they got to the ridge where they had first sighted smoke rising from the house, they stopped and looked back. They could not see anything for a while. The house was encircled by thick fog, which was most strange, as it had been very clear weather when they left. The fog hovered over the house and its surroundings as though hiding it, and at the last, it lifted. But the sisters never came out of the house to wave them on.

19

THE VILLAGE OF WEAVERS

They reached the Village of Weavers before sunset. People were coming home from their fields when they walked into the gate, and they were greeted by stares.

The headman too looked at them with no sign of recognition, until Pele said, 'It is I, Pele. This is Mesanuo and her son, Rhalietuo.'

'Pele! Is it really you? We thought you were all dead! Unbelievable! And who is this young man? Is this really your son, Mesanuo?'

'This is her son indeed,' Pele said to the headman, pushing the boy a little forward.

'No! Has he grown so big?'

Pele learned that they had been away close to seven years in the abandoned village. No wonder the headman could not recognize them. It was not surprising that people in the village had given them up for dead.

Since it was getting dark quickly, they headed to Mesanuo's house and went inside. She found an old kerosene lamp and lit it. They could see the interior of the house clearly now. A couple of mice ran across the kitchen floor, startling her.

A thick layer of dust covered everything. She took a broom and started to sweep, but the dust rose in thick clouds and made all of them cough.

'This won't do,' she said. 'It's best that I wash the house in the morning.'

Pele agreed, and tried to think of a solution. 'Why don't we all sleep in my house tonight? Or you two can sleep there and I will sleep at the headman's house.'

'Will your house be less dusty?' she asked.

'We'll see.'

The door was bolted from outside. It didn't look like anyone had tried to use the house in the years they had been away. But it was less dusty than Mesanuo's house; Pele used a damp rag to wipe off the dust on the chairs and the bed. He made a fire, cooked a simple dinner from the food they had with them, and they ate in silence. They were all very tired from their trip and the parting had made it an especially hard journey.

Pele made two beds for the mother and son, and he went across to the headman's house, seeking shelter for the night.

'Neisolie!' he called out, and the door was immediately opened.

'Come in, Pele, I have been waiting for you.' There was a fire burning in the hearth, but the other members of the household had gone to sleep.

'You were in the abandoned village all this time?' the headman asked.

'Yes, and the change is incredible. There is food growing outside the sisters' house. They neither plough nor sow, but the wind and the rain do it all for them. It was amazing.'

'They treated you well?'

Pele was surprised by this question. 'They were the most charitable hostesses I have ever known,' he said.

The headman nodded his head. 'People of the village fear them,' he said.

'Why? That is stupid. They mean no harm to anyone. They are not evil. They are only two very old women who, as they told me, had lived on hope, waiting for the prophecy to be fulfilled.'

'It is because of the prophecy that people fear them.'

'I don't understand what there could be to fear about the prophecy.' Pele was totally perplexed by what he was hearing.

'Not everyone has heard the prophecy the way you tell it. Not everyone hopes it will be fulfilled.' Pele could not believe his ears. How could a prophecy to save the village not be welcomed?

'Mesanuo looks different tonight. She looks like the tiger-widow again. Maybe she is very tired,' the headman remarked. He glanced at the dying light of the fire, and then turned back to Pele, who didn't answer him.

'Surely you don't believe the story that a raindrop fell on her and made her conceive a child?' The headman looked scornful as he said this.

'If that is not the real story,' Pele began carefully, 'what is the true version? What do you go by?'

'She had a lover. She must have had one; the whole village believes that now.'

'Have you forgotten how old she was? She would have been at least three hundred years old when she birthed the child and was changed. You think she had a lover? What vile mind could accept that?' Pele burst out angrily.

'People prefer to believe what is more plausible rather than what is miraculous,' the headman replied with an unpleasant look in his eyes.

There were many thoughts running through Pele's mind now. When he first entered the headman's house, he had had a desire to unload himself to another human being, but something now stopped him from doing that. I can't trust him anymore, he thought. He felt his stomach churn and form a hard knot. I can never tell him all.

20

PROPHECIES DIE IN THE FACE OF UNBELIEF

In the morning, Pele woke and watched the light grow through a crack in the window. He heard the voices of children, and slowly recalled the long walk down the hill from the abandoned village. He recollected going to sleep in the headman's house because he had given his house to Mesanuo and Rhalie. The conversation with the headman came back to him. *Not everyone has heard the prophecy the way you tell it. Not everyone hopes it will be fulfilled.* What did the man mean by that? He must question him again without rousing his suspicions.

He lay in bed, pondering everything that had happened in the recent past. He had no doubt that the sisters had now gone from their village. The last thing he had noticed was Kethonuo turning into ether, and Siedze looking almost transparent. The two sisters had been so anxious for them to leave. Why? Would it have been dangerous for them to be on the mountaintop without the sisters to protect them? He would ask Mesanuo about it later.

He heard muffled voices coming from the kitchen. He did not pay attention until he heard mention of Mesanuo. They referred to her as the tiger-widow.

'The boy has grown into a young man, and the tiger-widow has the traveller completely under her spell. Together they might be able to kill the tiger, and that would put us all in danger.' It was the headman's voice.

'Do you think so?' his wife asked timidly.

'Oh yes. Who do you think has been protecting our fields all these years since it rained? Was it not the tiger keeping other animals away and making sure we had good harvests so we could sacrifice to him? If they kill the tiger, we could be overtaken by famine again. Now, when everything is going so well, why did they have to return? Couldn't they have stayed on at the abandoned village with those two witches?'

'Hush, Neisolie. He might hear you,' his wife cautioned him.

Pele was horrified by what he had heard. He wondered

how much Mesanuo actually knew. Was this why she was reluctant to leave the safety of her sisters' house and return to the valley? There was so much hostility here. It was odd that he had never felt it before. Perhaps they had kept it well hidden. Either that or this was a new development after they had left. He recalled how the sisters had talked about Rhalie's destiny, and the fact that his goodness would be resented.

It was a rude shock to wake up among real people again, people with their petty minds thinking the worst of others. But it was not just that. There had been something downright malicious about the way the headman had said that everyone believed Mesanuo had had a lover. Pele was angry again. How could they, having lived with her for so long, and having seen her transformation, have no faith in the prophecy? And the headman mentioning something about sacrificing to the tiger—what was all that about?

He got up abruptly and went to the kitchen. The couple sprang apart guiltily. Had he overheard them? Pele gave no indication that anything was amiss.

'Ah that was a sound sleep if ever I have had one. I should go now. Thank you for your hospitality.'

'You mustn't go without a cup of tea, at least,' the woman insisted. She was already pouring out tea from a kettle into an enamel mug. Pele thanked her and sat down by the fire. On the excuse of getting more firewood, his host went out of the house.

'Tell me,' Pele asked his hostess, 'has anyone seen the tiger in our absence?'

She looked taken aback by his question and said, 'What tiger are you talking about?'

'You know, the one that killed the widow's husband and seven sons?'

'Oh that one,' she laughed nervously, 'everyone knows that is just a story. No one's ever seen the tiger and no one really believes that story anymore. Has she been telling you that?'

'No, I never heard that story from her. It was the others in this village who told me about it. And in the village I came from, we knew about it.' Pele looked directly into her eyes when he said that. She was most uncomfortable, and she looked away, and began to poke the fire.

'Well,' she began, trying to regain her composure, 'we'll be having a community hunt next month. If there is any tiger in these parts, our hunters can find him and put paid to the rumour.'

'Haha,' Pele laughed and finished his tea. He thanked her again and left.

For the first time, he felt unsafe in the village. He looked behind him before he entered his house. He saw no one but could not shake off the feeling that he was being watched.

'Rhalie!' he called as he entered his house. The boy was still sleeping but his mother was up and making food already.

'Didn't you sleep well?' he asked.

'To tell the truth, no. There was such a wind blowing outside and I kept waking up every time I dozed off. In the end, I sat up and kept watch over Rhalie while he slept.'

This was strange to hear, as there had been no wind blowing outside the headman's house, which was only two houses away. They looked at each other in unspoken understanding. There was something in the village that wanted to harm the boy. They felt the hostility of the villagers this time. It was barely concealed and they felt unwelcome. It made them question the wisdom of leaving the abandoned village.

'Should we have built another village beside it and stayed on?' Pele voiced his thoughts to Mesanuo when Rhalie was not around.

'No, we did the right thing. It will be better once the tiger is killed and his influence is broken over the people here.'

'Is it possible for them to make sacrifices to the tiger?' Pele asked.

'Pelevotso,' she said, using his full name, 'this is not a tiger of flesh and blood. It looks and acts like one, but it is really a spirit tiger. If the people of this village are sacrificing to it, it must have spread its influence while we were gone. You will need spiritual weapons to kill it. My son has his spear from my sisters. He can kill it with that, but not with just any other spear.'

'A specially made spear?'

'Yes. They stayed alive just long enough to give it to him. It's a spear point, not the whole spear. I carried it in my bag all the way here.'

'And I didn't know anything about it,' Pele smiled.

'I'm sorry. I had so many other things on my mind,' she explained. 'I was grieving over the final parting from my sisters and I forgot about it.'

'That was hard for you, wasn't it? But you are not alone. You won't be so long as I am alive,' he said. He was surprised by the intensity of his words. But he felt no shame or embarrassment.

Neither did she, and she smiled gratefully at him.

Rhalie stirred and opened his eyes. He saw Pele in the kitchen and got up quickly.

'Anie Pele, sorry I have been sleeping long. I was so tired,' he said.

'No need to apologize. It was a long journey. Have you slept well?'

'Oh yes. I was dreaming of Azuo Kethonuo and Azuo Siedze. They had grown wings and when I tried to catch up with them, they kept flying higher.'

When Rhalie stood there, Pele could see how big he had grown. He was almost as tall as his mother, and looked very much like her. The same bone structure, although he was beginning to develop the muscles of a man. He was a handsome boy, like a masculine version of his mother.

'They have gone, Rhalie, they are back where they

belong. Kethonuo was already half spirit when we were leaving. That's why she covered herself up in bed.' Pele admitted. He did not want to hide anything from his two friends. From now on, they would be completely honest with each other, and Rhalie was old enough to understand.

'I think it was what they wanted,' Rhalie said. 'I'd like to see them again one day.'

'And you will,' Pele said with conviction, 'life does not end here on earth. It actually begins with leaving the earth.'

'I'm so glad to hear you say that.'

21

THE TIGER

Pele whittled a shaft from a young, strong oak for Rhalie's spear. The flint point was not very long, and Pele worried that he might not get enough momentum to thrust at the tiger so that it could hit a strategic spot. But he also realized that he should have faith in the spear-point as it was especially fashioned for Rhalie to use against the tiger. He went back to whittling the shaft and making it as accurate as possible. He borrowed the spears of his neighbours to check and make sure that the alignment was just right.

'How's that?' he asked proudly when he was done, presenting the spear to its young owner.

Rhalie took it and turned it round and round. He pretended to thrust it at an imaginary foe. Rubbing the shining head, he said, 'It's splendid!'

'Does it feel all right? Not too heavy?' Pele asked anxiously.

'No, it's perfect for me,' Rhalie replied. He was lifting it up again and trying different moves with it. Pele handed him an oiled rag. 'Here, you can polish your spearhead with a little oil so that it looks really shiny.' The boy took the rag and immediately started to use it. When he was satisfied, he put the spear in a corner of his room, not far from his bed.

'Do you have a spear for yourself, Anie Pele?' he asked.

'I have two. You can borrow one when you want to practice with it,' he offered.

They were suddenly interrupted by a shout from outside. 'Rhalie!'

Someone was at the door, calling in a loud voice. Rhalie went to the door and opened it slowly. The young man who was standing at the door stepped into the house. He was shorter than Rhalie and Pele did not recognize him at all.

'A friend of yours?' he asked Rhalie in a loud voice. He was irritated at the young man's rudeness. Any young person visiting a family was expected to greet the elders of the house. The young man had walked in as though he owned the place, and totally ignored Pele. Pele's remark made him turn around and look a little abashed.

'Sorry, Anie, I didn't see you were there.' He was lying, but Pele decided not to point that out. 'I'm Viphrü, Neisolie's son,' he introduced himself.

Before Pele could react, Rhalie exclaimed, 'Viphrü! You've grown so big! I couldn't recognise you at all!' Turning to Pele, he explained, 'You'll remember, Anie Pele. We used to play together when we were smaller.'

Pele acknowledged that with a nod. He had no inclination to be friendly toward the insolent young man.

'There's a community hunt next month. You should come with us, in fact every man of this village is participating in it,' Viphrü announced.

'What are you going to hunt?' Rhalie asked.

'Stag, wolves, bear, tiger, whatever comes in our path. There are enough spears,' Viphrü declared rather arrogantly.

'I'll come too,' Rhalie replied, 'I have a spear now.' He pointed to the spear at his bedside.

'What? That old thing?' Viphrü scoffed. 'You'll never kill anything with that. I'll give you my spear. I have three.'

'This one is good enough for me,' Rhalie said. 'I don't know your spear, but I have confidence in mine and in the person who gave it to me.'

Viphrü laughed. It was not a pleasant sound.

'All right, bring that along and we'll see. And don't be upset if you don't get anything,' he ended with a spiteful little snigger. Then, without another word to either of them, he left.

'What an arrogant little scoundrel!' Pele exploded. 'If I catch him alone some night, and he tries to lord it over me, I'm going to throw him into the river.'

'He was never nice. I see he hasn't changed one bit,' Rhalie agreed.

'I don't like this community hunt one bit. I know it's unavoidable that we join it, but even if we go, make sure you are not around that young man. There is something nasty about him. He's jealous of you and will try to harm you if he gets the opportunity.'

'Do you think so?' Rhalie asked.

'I can see it etched all over him.'

Rhalie fetched his spear and lifted it to the light. The spearhead gleamed in the morning sun. He lightly rubbed his hand over it, and let out a little yelp. He had cut his finger on the point of the spear. A drop of blood fell off the tip. 'It's sharp enough,' he said and put it back.

'You know something? You and I should go out before the hunt and acquaint ourselves with the forest down here. We have lived so long up on the mountain that we have forgotten the terrain in the valley. Shall we do that?' Pele asked.

'What a good idea,' Rhalie agreed.

~

The next day they packed their mats, hunting knives and some food and left. Rhalie carried his spear but Pele took a bow and some arrows and a long-handled *dao*. They went across the river and followed the narrow path until it ended at the dense forest areas that were the hunting grounds for the villages in the area. Pele showed Rhalie how to set up a sitting place in a big tree, after checking that the wind was upwind of them.

'What next?' Rhalie asked.

'We will wait, and we must wait without making any noise at all. When a deer or a wild pig comes, you have to throw your spear quickly and kill it. Think you can do it?'

'Yes,' Rhalie said eagerly, and Pele saw in his eyes that he would indeed be able to do it.

They waited in their places on separate trees close to each other. It grew darker and darker, and the forest fell silent after some time. There was a thin new moon. They could make out shadows and outlines but otherwise it was too dark to see beyond a few metres. Even so, a pair of lights shone in the distance like two small stars. They glowed steadily and moved forward. Pele recognized it first. The tiger!

Could Rhalie kill it with his spear? Why hadn't he brought his own spear? Why had he been so foolhardy? Of course, the tiger was here. Hadn't the villagers been sacrificing to it?

Pele turned towards Rhalie, making frantic gestures, and Rhalie lifted his hand to indicate that he was aware of the danger. He had seen it from his place on the tree. He felt fear constrict him and choke him until he was unable to breathe. This was the tiger that had killed his father and brothers. He sucked in air noisily, but the animal was standing still. It was waiting.

The waiting was nerve wracking. Each hunter knew that the one who made the first move would make himself vulnerable to his foe. So they must wait. The longer he waited, the more Rhalie felt his flesh tremble and grow cowardly. I will wait no more, he thought to himself. I was born for this. The tiger knows it too, and it's trying to prevent me from acting. The next second he was down on the ground. As soon as he moved, the tiger pounced, swooping down on what it expected to be an easy prey. Rhalie was fearless the moment he jumped into action. He timed his every move and when he saw the great beast spring, he waited a few seconds before lifting his spear upward and holding it straight, swerving neither to the right nor to the left. The tiger fell heavily upon the spear. Its heart was pierced right through by the spearhead that was designed only for one purpose: to kill a spirit tiger.

'Rhalie!' Pele dashed from his place to the spot where he had seen the blurry movement of a great animal. His *dao* upraised to strike, he ran with his feet barely touching the ground. But it was done. Rhalie had killed the tiger, and he stood beside the fallen beast, panting and trembling.

'My son, you've done it! You have killed the tiger! It's over now.'

'Anie...' Rhalie managed to utter, but before he could finish his sentence he fainted.

22

THE HUNT

They came back to the village with the head of the tiger. It was massive.

'*Rhalietuo tekhu puo geilie ho!*' Pele shouted from time to time as they came within hearing distance of the village. It was the customary way to announce a tiger kill. *Rhalietuo has killed a tiger!*

The women stopped their cooking and pounding. '*Shie! Rhalietuo tekhu geilie shie!*' they said to each other, affirming the news they had heard, and they came running out to see. The men and children followed and helped the tiger-killer and his assistant carry the head to the village.

The headman was waiting at the gate and said, 'Do not come. You have killed our elder brother, do not come.' That was the traditional initiation of the many rituals of tiger killing. Pele whispered something to Rhalie who was now walking towards the gate. Rhalie repeated what Pele had whispered to him: 'It was not I, *Apfu-o*. It was the spear who killed Tiger.'

When he said that, the two of them were allowed to enter the village, where they were quickly surrounded by the few old men who were familiar with the rituals of tiger killing.

'Let him cook from a new fireplace for five days and eat separately, using a different set of pots and pans. He needs his clansmen to guard him for a week. But since he has no clansmen, we will guard him in turns,' they said.

Mesanuo was waiting for them at the entrance to her house. She was weeping tears of joy. Wordlessly she pulled her son inside and Pele followed them in.

'Ah my son, my son, the prophecy is fulfilled! And you have been spared to me. Oh! My life is beautiful again.' She laughed and cried and laughed again like a madwoman. 'Were you not a baby just yesterday, Rhalietuo? Son of the Thundercloud, what joy you have brought to all of us!'

She turned her beautiful tear-filled eyes to Pele and thanked him with glances because she had no words left that could express her gratitude.

They had to work on all the demands of the tiger

killing rituals. Rhalie had to make a new fireplace and cook in separate pots for himself. He also had to use freshly cut wood. They were fastidious about following all the instructions, for this was one way of showing they were interested in the welfare of the village. The three of them were not left alone for long. The old men came and met Rhalie, with more instructions to observe. The young men came and asked him to celebrate with them. Viphrü and four friends said they had three-day-old brew that Rhalie should share with them. Rhalie politely declined, saying that he could not touch anything alcoholic before the rituals were completed. The young men could not take offence at that.

In the village houses, they spoke of Rhalietuo, the young tiger-killer, and young girls his age felt the awakenings of first love at the mention of his heroic deed.

'Why don't you marry him instead of Viphrü?' they teased Vinuo, Viphrü's girlfriend.

The girl blushed and protested, 'Don't let Viphrü hear that, you know how jealous he gets.'

'Well, all the more reason to marry the tiger-killer instead,' they persisted.

Viphrü's sister was among the girls, and Vinuo knew whatever she said would be reported back to Viphrü. 'A man doesn't have to kill a tiger to win a girl's heart,' she said tactfully.

The next day she could tell Viphrü had heard of the

innocent teasing that the girls had been indulging in. He looked irritated and did not acknowledge her presence. When the girls were playing on the riverbank, Viphrü found her on her own and viciously pulled her hair from the back. She screamed in pain, and he let go and ran off. It was his way of warning her not to get interested in the tiger-killer.

Viphrü's jealousy of Rhalietuo ran very deep, but when they met in public, onlookers would be deceived into thinking that the two young men were the best of friends. Viphrü insistently invited Rhalie to be his companion on the hunt, promising to oil and polish an excellent spear for him to use; no onlooker could detect any sign of animosity.

When the tiger rituals were completed, Rhalie drank brew with Viphrü and his friends. He had tried every excuse to get out of it, but had to sit with them at least once to show that he was no enemy.

'All the girls like you now, tiger-killer,' Viphrü said in a boisterous tone. 'Do you like any of them?'

Rhalie was not sure how he was expected to answer. 'I do. They are all nice and pretty and kind,' he said.

'Any one in particular?' Viphrü persisted.

'I don't know them well. They are all equally nice, I think,' Rhalie said, trying to stay on safe ground.

'What if we told you to marry Vinuo, the one with the long, curly hair?'

'No. I don't want to marry any of them,'

'What? Are you too good for them?' Viphrü snapped.

'No, that is not what I mean. I love all of them, and I love all of you. How shall I explain it?' Rhalie felt helpless and trapped.

'You sound like a girl now,' Viphrü spat out in disgust. 'Go home, and get ready for the hunt. It's tomorrow.'

Their drinking ended abruptly, but Rhalie was relieved. They went their separate ways, Viphrü shouting after everyone not to be late for the hunt.

~

The next day, all the able-bodied men were assembled for the community hunt. Pele and Rhalie joined the men. They were divided into separate groups. The young men led by Viphrü would chase the animals up the hill where the older men would be waiting with their spears and bows and arrows.

The young men were called hunting dogs on these community hunts and Rhalie found himself in a group with Viphrü and his friends, going through the forest shouting and trying to find animals to chase up the hill. They eventually trapped a stag and chased it up, and the waiting men made an easy kill. Next they found tracks of a deer, and they began to shout from different directions in order to confuse the animal and flush it out into the open.

Rhalie was standing behind a tree that partially hid him from view. Viphrü shouted, 'There's the deer, strike him down. No point chasing him up. Let's get this one!' He threw his spear and it went through Rhalie's heart. With a grunt, he fell to the ground, unable to understand what was happening.

'Go on, hit it while it's down, can't you see it over there?' Viphrü goaded his friends, who threw their spears at the hapless boy on the ground. Some of them believed it was a deer, while the others clearly saw it was a boy, but they thought their eyes had tricked them, since all their friends were spearing the animal, and they too threw their spears at Rhalie's now lifeless body.

When all the boys had thrown their spears and every single one was a killer, Viphrü shouted, 'That's enough. Let's go get him.'

They ran up to the spot, and when they saw what they had done, all of them cried and tore their hair. But Viphrü said, 'No, it's not our fault. The spirits of the forest have tricked us; they deceived our eyes into seeing a deer where a man stood. We have to tell the elders what happened. Tell them the truth. Don't be afraid. Don't lie.'

When the hunting dogs stopped chasing up animals and were quiet for a long time, Pele and the headman went down to investigate. The first thing Pele glimpsed was the group of youths huddled over a figure. His heart beat fast as he foresaw what had happened. Still he prayed silently, let it not be him! He ran frantically down to the tree.

'No! Not this! Not this!' Pele shouted as the truth hit him. Rhalie's speared body lay on the grass beside the tree where he had been standing. His face was bloodless. Pele roared in anger at the young men. His eyes were red-rimmed as he ran from one to the other. He slapped them and shook them violently in his rage. The youths silently took their punishment, and then they began to speak, making entreaties and expressing their innocence. Pele turned around to look for Viphrü. There was a look of pure triumph fixed on his face, but when he felt Pele's eyes on him, it disappeared and sadness replaced it. Pele swung a fist at him, but the young man ducked. The other men, hearing Pele shouting, had already reached by then, and they held him and tried to calm him down.

The headman spoke. 'This is a great tragedy, traveller. Take his body home to his mother. Let two boys help you. I will come by and explain. We have to suspend the community hunt now.'

Pele bent down to remove the spears from Rhalie's body. He refused to accept help from the boys. Carefully wrapping Rhalie in a cloth, Pele lifted him on his shoulder and carried him home to the village.

23

GRIEF

Mesanuo was standing at the doorway. She saw Pele walking into the village with a burden. At first she thought it was a deer. But she saw the feet that stuck out of the cloth and hung limply down. Realization dawned, and she wailed loudly as she ran to hold her son's body.

'Rhalietuo! What have they done to you?'

'Let me take him inside the house,' Pele pleaded.

'No, place him here in the middle of the village. Let them all see my grief!' Mesanuo cried loudly. 'Let them see what their sons have done to my child!'

Her cries brought the women running out of their

homes. They wept with her, the ones who genuinely loved the boy.

Mesanuo was beside herself with grief. 'Look what they have done to my son. He saved you, he saved the whole village from the tiger, and your sons have killed him!' She shouted at the mothers.

'How can I say how sorry I am! I should have kept him by my side,' Pele was saying.

'No, it's not your fault. They would have killed him anyway, if not there today, some other place, some other day,' she said through her tears, 'I knew it, but how hard it is to bear.'

She opened the cloth to look at her son. He was very pale and very still. His face looked like that of an angel.

A second time Pele asked to carry the body into the house, and finally she said he might. He gently lifted the boy in his arms and carried him into his mother's house. She had already laid out a bed in the first room. So it was true, she had known all along, thought Pele.

After that outburst of sorrow, Mesanuo reined in her anguish and went about the preparations for the dead. She washed her son's body with lukewarm water, getting all the congealed blood out where the spear points had been thrust into his flesh. She closed the wounds with muslin cloth and bound them. She washed his face and arms and legs and asked Pele to cover him with a new body-cloth. Pele had gone through the task of bringing the body back in a mechanical way. He had stopped feeling in order to bring the boy home to his mother. Now that she had bathed him and everything was made ready, he wept as though his heart would break. He wept in anger, he wept in loss, he wept at his impotence to stop this happening.

People were beginning to gather at the house. The girls brought fresh flowers and placed them at the foot of the bed. Older women came in calling out his name and praising him and mourning him in the traditional way. One by one, they held Mesanuo and she wept afresh in their embrace. But once the chanting stopped, she controlled herself and sat by his side, calling his name over and over. '*Thia zie nza kie salhote*,' she said, lamenting the fact that this day was the last day she would call his name.

The skies which had been so clear and blue in the morning turned cloudy and grew overcast. The hunters had straggled home, with the stag that they had killed, quartered and brought to the village without any ceremony.

The young men wanted to come and pay their respects but Mesanuo would not allow it. 'Don't let them come anywhere near my son. If they try, I will personally pierce their hearts through,' she told Pele, and he conveyed the message to them. They didn't ask again after that.

Mesanuo would go into her room calling out to her sisters and her son, and return and sit beside her son, sometimes laying her head on his chest. Pele kept his lonely vigil by the dead boy, calling his name aloud from time to time as was the custom for mourning the dead.

Where should he be buried? The headman and the other elders wanted to discuss that with Pele so that he could tell the mother.

'Not here,' Mesanuo interrupted them. 'I want to take him to the abandoned village and bury him there.'

When he first heard it, Pele thought it was absurd. But when he thought it over, he could understand why she would want that. These people had killed her son, their sons were guilty, but the parents were just as guilty because they had allowed their sons to believe in a lie. Why should the boy be buried amongst people who had hated him in life? Pele spoke to the headman, and demanded that four of the men bear up the body in a coffin all the way to the abandoned village. 'It is the least that the village can do,' he said. The headman readily agreed and found four volunteers. They would leave in the morning. Mesanuo was satisfied with the arrangement. She busied herself in the house, packing things away. It was clear she was not going to return.

'Why?' Pele asked.

'This part of my life is over. I cannot return to live here. I don't know what I will do but I will make my home where my son is buried.'

The rain came at night, a monster rainstorm that ruined houses and fields and flooded the river so that all arable lands were swallowed by the deluge. The fields of full-eared grain were smashed to the ground, the stalks broken so that the grain would never ripen. The roofs of houses were torn off and the signs of devastation were the last sights of the Village of Weavers when the burial party left early the next morning with their burden. They climbed up the hill, and kept climbing until Mesanuo asked them to stop.

'Here,' she said, pointing to a spot that overlooked the valley. 'I want to bury him here.' The men laid down the coffin and dug the soil wide enough for the coffin to be lowered. When they were finished, they bowed to her and went back down the path without saying a word.

'It is done. I won't have to wait long, dear friend.' Mesanuo smiled wanly at Pele.

'May I ask what is going to happen next?'

'I have finished what I was supposed to do on earth,' Mesanuo began. 'I was to mother a son, not from the dust of the earth, but from rain, because water is the purest form of life you can find. It is a metaphor for true love. He would teach people how to love.

'The Village of Weavers forgot who their real enemy was. They were worshipping the tiger and sacrificing to their enemy, and they killed my son because he had killed the tiger. They were consumed by hate. They hated others, but when you hate someone, you are really hating yourself and hurting yourself. Perhaps now they will learn to change; perhaps now they will stop hating.

'Try to understand, my friend, there is still that much of the flesh left in me that makes the thought of living in that village abhorrent to me. Among people who hated a child so much that they killed him.'

'I understand that, Mesanuo,' Pele said. 'I won't go back either.'

24

THE ABANDONED VILLAGE

They walked towards the abandoned village. The house was still standing but the trees around looked thin and stunted, as though the tops had been sheared off.

Everything else was unchanged. They stood outside the house, and waited a little, as if needing permission to enter. Mesanuo finally pushed the door open and went in; Pele followed after her. It was strange not to find the two sisters there. The house looked big and empty.

Mesanuo went from room to room, touching every item, brushing a hand over the beams, pulling a window shut.

'They are gone, of course. I didn't expect to find them

here. Perhaps it is instinct that brings us back to a place where we've been happy. I want to stay here. I want to make this my home for the rest of my life on earth.'

'It's a good decision. There's the taboo about living in an abandoned village, but how would it harm you any further?'

'But look around—there's no sign that this is an abandoned village. Look at it, it's fertile and verdant. There's enough food here to feed several villages...'

'Rename it,' Pele interrupted her.

'Rename what?' she asked absent-mindedly.

'This village here. Call it by another name.'

'Ah yes. It used to be called Noune before. Noune means Peace. But I don't think it's a good omen to give a village its old name again. I shall call it Nouzie, compassion. I shall name it in memory of my son's compassionate heart. He loved everyone, even those who harboured evil against him.' Her voice broke at this last sentence.

'It's a good name, Mesanuo. You have come to a good place. A place of compassion.'

They found food outside the house and brought it in before it got dark. Pele made a fire and when darkness came, the stars seemed brighter than before. Now they could no longer watch the stars from inside the house with its new roof, so they went outside after they had eaten. They stood side by side and began to count the stars.

'There's a new star, look!' he pointed at a spot low on the horizon. She saw it immediately, a young star hanging just above the mountains, on the very rim of the blue-black world.

'Maybe that's someone we both know,' Pele smiled.

'Because they say good people turn into stars when they die?' she asked.

'Why wouldn't it be him? If others who were half as good as him have turned into stars after they died, why not him?'

Pele said this with such hope in his voice that she teared up. 'Why not indeed, dear friend.'

The new star was not very bright. Sometimes they couldn't see it, and then, even as they stood there scanning the skies and thinking their eyes had deceived them, they would see it again, twinkling dimly. It was certainly there, if they looked long enough. They stood outside, quite oblivious of time, watching this lone new star, feeling comforted every time they saw it, their deep shared sorrow soothed by every sighting.

Mesanuo was the first to turn back toward the house. 'We can come out tomorrow and watch again,' she said.

'Yes, we can. And we will.'

The house was in darkness and the faint light from the fire was all that was visible. They walked back slowly, careful to keep to the narrow track, as they had gone beyond the chasm to look at the star. When they were at the house, Pele opened the door. To their surprise it was brighter inside than they expected. He stoked the fire with more wood until it lit up the whole house.

'To think we were here just a couple of months ago, and Kethonuo was sitting right there and Siedze over there with Rhalie beside her. They had such a special bond those two,' Mesanuo sighed as the memories came back afresh to her.

'Be grateful you had that time together,' Pele said, then corrected himself: 'that we had that time together.'

'You're right,' she sighed again.

'You are tired. Would you like to lie down?'

'In a little while.'

He made her bed as comfortable as possible, piling the bed clothes she had brought atop the old ones left behind by her sisters.

Pele lay awake by the fire when Mesanuo had gone to bed. This was the first time he was alone after all that had happened in the last few days. He let his mind be stilled by the silence of the place, and the sound of the wind outside.

What would he do now? Where would he go? Of one thing he was very sure: as long as Mesanuo was alive, he would devote himself to looking after her. She should not suffer any more; she had already gone through so much.

There was a slight movement at the door. He did not look up, thinking it was just the wind. It came again and he sat up this time. The three of them stood at the door, smiling at him, Kethonuo, Siedze and Rhalie. He felt no fear, and smiled back. He sat there expectantly, waiting for them to reveal some mysterious knowledge, as they would in the past. But there was nothing of that. They smiled as though they were blessing him, and then they went away. Pele lay in bed and waited but they did not return. He couldn't remember falling asleep, but when he awoke he felt the silence that had settled over the house. He got up and splashed water on his face and went to see if Mesanuo had woken up.

She was lying on her back. Pele thought he would let her sleep a little longer, but then thought she might want to watch the sun rise over the valley. The sight would make her happy.

'Mesanuo,' he whispered. There was no response. He called her a couple of times more and when she did not stir, he went closer and looked. She had passed on. She looked very peaceful, as though her last sight of earth had been a beautiful one.

As he watched, he felt as though his heart were being ripped out of his chest. He wept loud and long, but while his heart wept, his mind told him this was right and as it should be. Now she would be with her loved ones, her sisters, and the son she loved more than life.

25

TRAVELLER

He buried her in the soft loamy soil of the earth that he had witnessed being regenerated by the miracle of thunder and rain. He shaped the earth into a mound over which the grass would grow and warn travellers that there was a grave there. Then he lifted his bag and walked out of the village that he would remember for the rest of his mortal days as Nouzie. Compassion.

At the ancient gate of the village he paused and knelt. His spirit felt the sacredness of the place. It was hallowed ground. He didn't want anyone to come and violate it. He said a prayer of three words: 'Protect it, please.'

Pelevotso then rose and took the path that would take him past Rhalietuo's grave on the hill overlooking the valley. He felt like he was the last man on earth. But there was a sense of closure about the last death; that was how it was meant to be. They belonged together, and his destiny was to be part of their life, briefly. No matter how much he loved her, he could never have replaced what she had lost, or made her forget her great sorrow. Perhaps there would be another star over the mountains tonight. They would always be together now.

Easterine Kire is a poet, novelist, short-story writer and writer of children's books. Her first novel, *A Naga Village Remembered*, was also the first Naga novel in English to be published. Her other novels include *Bitter Wormwood* (shortlisted for the Hindu Prize 2013) and *When the River Sleeps* (winner of the Hindu Prize 2015).

Easterine Kire's work has been translated into German, Croatian, Uzbek, Norwegian and Nepali. In 2011 she was awarded the governor's medal for excellence in Naga literature.